IAN TAYLOR

IN THEIR OWN WORDS

Radiohead

RADIOHEAD...IN THEIR OWN WORDS

Exclusive distributors:
Music Sales Limited
8-9 Frith Street, London W1D 3JB, UK
Music Sales Corporation
257 Park Avenue South, New York, NY 10010, USA
Macmillan Distribution Services
53 Park West Drive, Derrimut, Vic 3030, Australia
Exclusive distributors to the music trade only:
Music Sales Limited
8-9 Frith Street, London W1D 3JB, UK

ISBN 0.7119.9167.7
Order No. OP48752

Front cover: Steve Double/Retna; All Action: 57,58,84,100;
Redferns: 94; Rex: 61,76,104. All other pictures supplied by
London Features International.

Every effort has been made to trace the copyright holders of
the photographs in this book but one or two were unreachable.
We would be grateful if the photographers concerned would
contact us.

Cover and Book designed and originated by **Hilite**

Picture research by Nikki Lloyd, Omnibus Press

The author would like to thank Gaynor Edwards for her invaluable
research assistance on this project.

Printed in Great Britain

www.omnibuspress.com

OMNIBUS PRESS

Jonny

thom

Radiohead have had plenty of labels thrown at them over the years, ranging from champagne socialists to progressive rock. The truth is they are a hard band to pigeonhole, even if you wanted to. Endlessly experimenting, they themselves deny any grand masterplan and seem to have a limited idea as to what may or may not happen next.

Having spent more than a decade together as Radiohead, they are a testament to lasting friendship. The mutual respect that's existed since they came together at their Oxfordshire public school is undoubtedly the factor that has helped them develop individually into accomplished musicians and collectively into the band they are today.

Originally known as On A Friday, they put their collective career on hold while members completed their education – singer Thom Yorke set off for Exeter University to read Fine Art & Literature and guitarist Ed O'Brien to Manchester to do Politics, while the rhythm section of Colin Greenwood (bass) and Phil Selway (drums) studied English at Cambridge and Liverpool respectively.

In the summer of 1991 the members of On A Friday found themselves back together in Oxford. Colin, Ed and Phil rented a semi-detached house near the town centre, and this quickly became their base. They were soon joined by Colin's younger brother Jonny, now a fully-fledged keyboard player and guitarist. The scene was set for success – yet this was a band that almost went down in the annals of rock as one-hit wonders. Though their loser anthem 'Creep', a transatlantic Top 10 hit in 1993, became an albatross round their necks, they came back to confound the sceptics two years later with an inspirational second album, *The Bends*.

1997's *OK Computer* was voted second greatest British album ever behind The Beatles' *Revolver* when *Q* magazine celebrated the turn of the millennium with a survey of critics. And while the wilfully obscure *Kid A* caused controversy that very year, 2000, the release just months later of *Amnesiac*, a collection of more conventional songs from the same sessions, effortlessly re-

established their commercial standing. They'd shown the rock business they intended to participate on their own terms – a fact underlined by a tour in a marquee tent which was as far away from the corporately-sponsored mainstream as possible.

Now in their thirties, and with Yorke a proud father, they have never bought into the rock'n'roll lifestyle, viewing it as outdated and even contemptible. Although hardly devoid of emotion, they are a band ruled by the head, not the heart – as evidenced by their decision to go to university, never doubting they would return to the band and make a career of it.

They cite thinking too much as one of their biggest faults. Indeed, they have accentuated this angle to give them an easier ride, assuming a 'nerdy' image that has helped the individual members keep a low profile despite Radiohead's commercial success. Lead vocalist Yorke has almost inevitably had a few run-ins with the British press, but successfully rode the storm. Ultimately their egos have never got in the way of the music and Radiohead remain five blokes with a good ear for sound – in whatever form they choose to present it.

Childhood

I remember being eight years old, telling my guitar teacher that I was going to be a rock star and the teacher laughing his head off.
Thom (1993)

I was a sickly child. The content of my lyrics shows that I am almost obsessed with my health. If I get ill on tour, it really does something to me emotionally. I just can't go anywhere in that state.
Thom (1995)

When we started our little band, when we were kids at school, it was never really about being friends or anything. We were playing our instruments in our bedrooms and wanted to play them with someone else and it was just symbiotic. We never really thought about it.
Thom (1995)

People are born with certain faces, like my father was born with a face that people want to hit. I do stamp my feet out of frustration really, but I don't do it as much now because I feel that we're in more control of what's happening.
Thom (1995)

There's a pervading sense of loneliness I've had since the day I was born. Maybe a lot of other people feel the same way, but I'm not about to run up and down the street asking everybody if they're as lonely as I am. I'd probably get locked up.
Thom (1995)

When I was 18 I worked in a bar, and this madwoman came in and said, 'You have beautiful eyes but they're completely wrong.' Whenever I get paranoid, I just think about what she said.
Thom (1995)

One of the first things he (Thom's father) ever bought me was a pair of boxing gloves. He used to try to teach me to box, but whenever he hit me I'd fall flat on my arse.
Thom (1995)

When I was younger, I was in the music room most of the time, anyway. It was great. no-one came down and there were these tiny rooms with sound-proofed cubicles. I suppose I'm quite an aggressive person. I was a fighter at school, but I never won. I was into the idea of fighting. I've had to calm down a bit, otherwise I'd go nuts.
Thom (1997)

In my first year at college I went through this phase where I was into this granddad hat and coat I had. They were immaculate and I was into dressing like an old man. But I went out one night and there was these three blokes, townie guys, waiting to beat someone up and they found me. They said something, I turned around, blew them a kiss and that was it. They beat the living shit out of me. That put me off fighting a bit.
Thom (1997)

There was this tense dress rehearsal (for a school play) and Thom and this other fella were jamming freeform cod jazz throughout it. The director stopped the play and shouted up to this scaffold tower thing they were playing on, trying to find out what the hell was going on. Thom started shouting down, 'I don't know what the fuck we're supposed to be playing'. And this was to a teacher.
Ed (1997)

I found a book full of half-finished crosswords when I was 16. My father died when I was five or six. It was half filled out by him, so I used that as the basis for understanding how to do them. I've still got it somewhere. It's massively anal – it's kind of doubly satisfying, filling out a grid, and solving these massively witty clues.
Jonny (1998)

Early Years

Oxford is such a weird place and it's very important to my writing.
Thom (1991)

People sometimes say we take things too seriously, but it's the only way you'll get anywhere. We're not going to sit around and wait and just be happy if something turns up. We are ambitious. You have to be.
Thom (1991)

The rest of the band are basically Colin's friends. So it was me following them around and begging them to let me be in their band for two or three years. And they finally let me in on the harmonica, actually, and then the keyboards, and finally the guitar.
Jonny (1993)

It was at a crossing point in my songwriting. Because I'd gone from writing songs in my bedroom to being somebody who had huge record-company figures over my shoulders listening to me.
Thom (1993)

We were always going to do music, but the only vagueness was what shape the band would take and what future we had. There was never any sort of plan for signing or anything, but there was always a plan to write songs together, in one form or another. We just ended up being more and more in one another's company and relying on music and relying on being in the band for, for everything really, and ended up kind of getting obsessed with it.
Jonny (1993)

We just started making tapes when we were younger. First me on my own, and then me and Jonny, and then with the others. And we'd play them to people, and they'd really like them and they'd take them home and they'd actually play them at home and I was really into this. Or I'd be at a party or something and someone would give me a guitar and I'd play a song. I mean this is all when we were sort of 15, 16 and it was the first time that I found something that I really loved. I suppose I wanted to be famous, I wanted the attention.
Thom (1995)

Whenever anyone puts a microphone in front of me, I'm serious because I want to get these noises out of my head. At home I've got a very puerile, juvenile sense of humour. The people that make me laugh more than anyone else are Jonny and Ed. We've known each other since we were 15, so how can you not mercilessly rip the shit out of each other? It's just like when you're a kid; it's no different.
Thom (1995)

We weren't the school band in the sense of playing to all our friends at parties. We wrote songs and played for five years but not really in public more than once a year. **Jonny (1995)**

We started at a time when the shoegazing bands were big. They'd just stand there on stage looking at their shoes. Electronic dance music was also big then. The British rock scene had become sedate

We spent maybe five or six years trying out different musical styles, rehearsing in village halls, not playing for anyone, just for ourselves and occasionally a few friends. We balanced it very well. We all wanted to go to college but yet there was a total commitment to the band. There was never a question of us really not having a go of it after college. **Ed (1995)**

and apathetic. We began out of sheer boredom. **Ed (1995)**

It took five years to learn how to play. We were in the same room, but we weren't necessarily playing together. **Thom (1995)**

We had an argument over the name. Radiohead is the name of a song off Talking Heads' *True Stories* album; it's the least-offensive track. And 'Pablo Honey' is from a skit by the Jerky Boys. **Colin (1995)**

My advice is that if you're in a band and you feel good, stick with it and work at it, because basically what

we've done is kept a school band together for years with nothing happening – until recently.
Phil (1996)

We've been very tolerant in recognising good ideas in each other. The whole leap in terms of conception to actually performing makes it slightly laborious; we've cut each other lots of slack that

varying styles of haircut and demeanour which would now be openly laughed at in the street.
Colin (1997)

One track, 'Rattlesnake' (an early effort), just had a drum loop that Thom did himself at home on a tape recorder with bad scratching over the top and kind of Prince vocals … After hearing it, I knew Thom was

way. The intuitive side has benefited very much from ten years of playing together.
Phil (1996)

The thing about having been together for such a long period is that there are some heinously embarrassing group shots from ten years ago; adolescence with

writing great songs and I knew what I wanted to do.
Jonny (1997)

You know, the big thing was signing at the end of '91, then in '92 touring around in a rusty white van. It was great to do small shows, opening up for people. 1993 – the first half of the year was really the same as '92,

then of course 'Creep' erupted, and we came over here (to the US). 'Creep' was not what we expected. We all thought (progress) would be slow – we didn't want any kind of big explosion. We wanted to, each time you do a gig, a few more people come along, word of mouth spreads, make a better record…
Ed (1998)

We started off as a school band so there's always been a slight insecurity generated by that. Part of it is us saying over and over again to ourselves, 'Who are we trying to kid?'
Phil (2001)

At first it wasn't any big deal. I just thought, Oh Thom's doing songs that sound as good as Elvis Costello and R.E.M.. That's why it held my interest. I don't remember thinking anything would come of it. It was just music that was really good to make.
Jonny (2001)

Radiohead is very challenging. You are working with the same people you've been working with since school. Not that we've become set in our ways, but it can be a little difficult to see other ways at some points.
Phil (2001)

The important thing for me, apart from the friendship, was the quality of Thom's songs. I remember an acoustic version of 'Creep' he sent me a cassette of from Exeter University in 1987. I listened to it and said, 'This is what I want to do. This is my destiny: to help disseminate this music and propel it directly into contemporary popular culture because it is so important.'
Colin (2001)

We kept missing out on all the so-called movements – like shoegazing, Brit-pop and all that. We were so annoyed; it was like we'd arrived too late for everything.
Jonny (2001)

Boys In The Band

Thom

He can be quite, ummm, childish, I guess. And he's very creative. But not a creep, exactly.
Ed (1993)

Like the rest of the band, he sort of doesn't have any friends, really – which is a bit weird. We got back to Oxford after touring… and it was really sad. We all got home, and I phoned up one or two people that we knew, who were away, and then we ended up phoning each other up again.
Jonny (1993)

There was this tradition of leaders of Mesopotamia or somewhere of cutting themselves in public and sacrificing their own blood and throwing themselves into the audience. And maybe Thom is doing that. But probably not. **Jonny (1995)**

I'm not really serious, it's just when people get me on the subject of music. I think most bands do take themselves seriously but there's this double-think where you can be a musician but at the same time it's a bit of a joke.
Thom (1995)

Thom doesn't like to feel satisfied. When things are going well, he will throw things off balance so that he'll be in state of flux. That's the way he works best.
Phil (1995)

I suppose I draw my drum parts mainly from Thom; he's got a very good sense of rhythm.
Phil (1996)

We don't draw the curtains of our bedrooms at night when we're going to sleep and see all these people staring up at the window. We don't have to deal with that. It's different graduations of stress, I suppose. What's important to Thom is, if he can have two different personas, it's a way of protecting himself.
Colin (1997)

It's weird to see the public representation of Thom because it's quite different. I find Thom to be very affectionate and child-like. **Jonny (1997)**

I shared a room with Thom for four years, and that's not the man in the interviews.
Phil (1997)

Thom does the lyrics and usually kicks off the song, writes the majority of it or a tiny part of it. Things just get extended, altered and butchered by the rest of us. **Jonny (1998)**

Most of the reading is done by Thom. He is much more interested in ideological and philosophical subjects than the rest of us, and I think that in all probability this affects the way in

which he thinks and writes songs. We are not trying to sell our thoughts through our site. The stuff that appears there is only indicative of the things that affect us at a certain time, and is somehow mixed with the process of making an album.
Phil (2000)

What people don't understand is that Thom just doesn't like the scrutiny he comes under when he's interviewed. I think that's fair enough. Why do you have to do it? You don't.
Ed (2000)

I end up in our studio collaborating all the time. Walking into a situation cold and walking out again, that's my role. It makes me really happy because I have such a short attention span, but one of the things I'm good at is being able to spark people off.
Thom (2000)

Thom's got quite a legacy with the music press. I think in 1995 his face was on the cover of a magazine with the words: 'Is this going to be the next rock'n'roll suicide?' Why do you think he doesn't want to talk to people? I think he's got better things to do with this time. We haven't cut ourselves off, because of our website. We correspond with people through that. That's our outlet.
Ed (2000)

I don't hate myself quite as much as I used to – which I think is a bonus, really. Because that can only last so long without it destroying you.
Thom (2000)

He has a great art-school ethic. He did art at university and he has that kind of drive… I think I can be vaguely objective about this, and I think Thom is in the line of the John Lennons, the David Bowies, part of that heritage. He has an incredible gift.
Ed (2000)

Part of Thom's thing over the last three years was him wanting to change direction. He felt like a boxer hemmed into a corner, on the ropes. Those sessions were the first time that he did not produce lyric sheets for us when we were rehearsing.
But we rehearsed before Christmas, playing some new stuff, and, hey, there was a lyric sheet there! It was the first time in four years. It was like, 'Now that's good to see!'
Ed (2001)

Jonny

I don't think I could play anything fresh if I've heard it 100 times before. It wouldn't be dangerous, and there'd be no chance of it going wrong.
Jonny (1995)

Thom writes these songs that sound like a slightly more sinister Elvis Costello, then I come in and add extra structures and chords to make it more interesting. I have such a low boredom threshold that I need something more than good songs to keep my attention.
Jonny (1995)

Jonny's got all this mad shit that's got nothing to do with electric guitar. He joined the band when he was 14 and he was already a multi-instrumentalist even then. He can play keyboards and write string instruments. He can even read music. Actually, they all can now, except for me. Everything he picks up he can make music on. It's totally logical that he should be trying other things.
Thom (2001)

It's not about being a guitarist in a rock band, it's about having an instrument in front of you and you're really excited by it. It's like with Jonny playing his Ondes Martenot (instrument) on… just about everything! We couldn't stop him! We had to beg him to play guitar on 'Morning Bell'.
Thom (2001)

Colin

He (Colin) loves to go to all those dinners and wear bow ties. You've got to print that because he'll kill me. Yeah, he loves all that. In fact, his favourite thing is to have these dinners where everyone starts speaking in Latin and throwing food at each other. He loves all that.
Thom (1996)

Colin Greenwood's the one who got the degree in English from Cambridge, for which I'll be eternally jealous because he got in and I didn't. I did English literature and fine art.
Thom (1996)

novello
award

The Music

The best way to describe our music is thick pop. There's definitely a pop sensibility to it, but also a heavy guitar effect.
Ed 1995

Singles

'Creep'
Nobody knew at the time it would be a hit. It was the first thing we ever recorded. We've since tried to escape from that song, but it was the reason a lot of people came to see us in the first place.
Ed (1995)

I never want to set myself up like that again. I've had letters from Death Row, guys who have killed people, and they're responding in what they think is a positive way to the lyrics on 'Creep'. That really scared the hell out of me.
Thom (1995)

'Fake Plastic Trees'
Usually we write a song all together, compose it as a whole. That was done by Thom just playing by himself, gradually adding one thing at a time. It's all very considered, in a good way.
Jonny (1995)

The day we recorded that song was a complete nightmare – I had a complete meltdown, so everyone left the studio. It was just me and my acoustic guitar, but there was something chilling hanging around in the air. We'd been there for a month, and that was the first time I felt any connection with what Radiohead's about.
Thom (1995)

'Street Spirit (Fade Out)'
I'll never forget the moment we captured 'Street Spirit'. That stands out for me. The whole reason to be doing this is to arrive at those moments. It makes it worth all the scratching around for months on end in notebooks and all the hundreds of thousands of ideas you compile on endless tapes.
Thom (2001)

'Paranoid Android'
One of the proudest moments for me was getting 'Paranoid Android' on Radio 1. The reaction it got was just fucking wicked. Just amazing. You couldn't listen to it a lot on Radio 1. Each time I'd hear it, I'd keep thinking about people doing intricate jobs in factories – working on industrial lathes - getting injured from the shock of being exposed to it.
Thom (2001)

'No Surprises'
We were saying, 'Let's do it really straight ahead, let's not fuck around and spend ages analysing the material'. And we ended up doing 16 versions of 'No Surprises' and then went back to the first one. The problem is, we get bored very easily.
Ed (1998)

'Lucky'

There wasn't that sense of screaming and fighting and being on the phone to people for ages and spitting and swearing any more, I don't think. There was a sense of release to me, that was the thing I wanted. To me, 'Lucky' was sort of like that. 'Lucky' is a song of complete release. It just happened, writing and recording it, there was no time, no conscious effort.
Thom (1995)

Albums

Pablo Honey

There are at least five what I consider to be really good songs on the album. And even the ones that don't work so well still sound very good live, I think. They weren't recorded perfectly, but we're happy with the whole album. We're keen for it to be treated as a whole album, not just something that happens to have 'Creep' on it.
Jonny (1993)

Pablo Honey is all a reflection of us. It's cynical and nervous, and it doesn't make sense. And you get the feeling at the end of it that something's wrong, but you can't quite work out what.
Thom (1995)

We figured to sell 20,000 of *Pablo Honey*, which would be enough so that we would get to make another album. And we would be left alone to make it in our own way. Instead, we had to follow this big album and

also demonstrate in the process that we were a band of substance.
Jonny (1995)

We didn't feel it was a successful album. It had a successful song, but it wasn't a successful album.
Thom (1996)

The Bends

It is a dark album and it would have been a lot darker if we'd released the tracks that we'd first recorded. We were going around calling it 'The Heavy Mother Of An Album'. It reflected the atmosphere in the studio as well. I wouldn't say… the songs are down, but there's a sense of liberation in songs that are

melancholy that you relate to. In my teens, when I was listening non-stop to The Smiths, I thought it was quite funny and I also found it very uplifting, and I think there's definite traits of that in our music.
Ed (1995)

The reason I'm proud of the fact that people have jumped to *The Bends* now is because I know how difficult it was to make. The record is a document of a period of time and that was a difficult period of time and the fact that people really like it makes me very proud. I don't really care who wins Brit Awards because nobody else does.
Thom (1995)

It's inevitable that people look at us like a one-hit wonder, because that's all they know of us. But 'Creep' came along eight years into our existence; we've always been progressing. I think *The Bends* puts 'Creep' in its proper place. I'm sure there were some record company people who would've been happy with an album of 'Creeps'. But we've always been pretty diverse with our music.
Phil (1995)

In making this album, it was very much a case of re-focusing on what we enjoyed musically after all the hype and insanity from the first album. When that all died down, we found that Thom had written a terrific bunch of songs, and we wanted to do them justice.
Phil (1995)

I'd say it's a cohesive guitar-based album that works really well together. The songs just flow and work well with one another.
Colin (1995)

When you meet people it's a different thing. People put pen to paper for different reasons, some of them quite weird. It was set up like that from the first record because of 'Creep' and all the hyperbole around that, but actually we lost most of that debris when we brought out *The Bends*. Murderers have stopped writing to me to say how much they can relate to 'Creep', so that's cool. Now it's just people who're into what we're doing and there's respect on both sides.
Thom (1997)

OK Computer

I think the third album will be celebratory and maybe not so inward-looking, that would be great. I think thinking is a good thing but there are times when you say 'Fuck it'. We're allowed to make mistakes.
Ed (1995)

I suppose that was the bit that was really exciting – doing something you've spend so long on and really agonised about, really having this sound in our heads, like the sound of Ed's guitar on the beginning of 'No Surprises' or the way 'Airbag' starts. One sounds like a car accident, the other sounds like a child's toy. And for people to pick up on those things was a real fucking kick. Really cool.
Thom (1998)

I suppose it was quite well-received, but we did wonder if it might have turned us into a one-trick band.
Phil (2000)

I obviously can't listen to it (*OK Computer*), I have to listen to it to remember the songs. But I can't do that. It really freaks me out. I can't do it.
Thom (2000)

When we did *OK Computer*, all the vocals were first takes because (a) I couldn't do it again afterwards and (b) it was about being in the moment. The lyrics are gibberish but they come out of ideas I've been fighting with for ages about how people are basically just pixels on a screen, unknowingly serving this higher power which is manipulative and destructive, but we're powerless because we can't name it.
Thom (2001)

I think *OK Computer* was a song too long. With our music, 45 minutes is enough. That's all the human ear can take.
Ed (2001)

Kid A

It seems music has got to the point where everybody has the right to go any place they like. And it shouldn't be over your career or one record, it can be over a song, or even ten seconds. There's ten

seconds of hip-hop on the LP, Y'know. To me that's how I listen to music now. I don't want to be in a rock band any more, anyway.
Thom (2000)

The interesting thing about bands and music is the way they develop. I think in a couple of albums' time, *Kid A* will be seen as more important than it is now. It's another way of working, it's another methodology. That's what's interesting, and that's what was interesting about Bowie in the Seventies or Lou Reed or whoever. Sometimes you have to just trust your instincts.
Ed (2000)

It's as though a lot of people were secretly hoping we'd make a record that sounded like all the people who sound like us. That would have just been pointless.
Jonny (2000)

What's been great is that a lot of musicians have come up to us and said they like elements on the record. That's what it's about.
Ed (2000)

What we're hearing in our heads is much more like this disjointed, fragmented thing, very much a landscape. Well, the artwork is very much a landscape – for fear of sounding prog-rocky. It wasn't about people as such, not really about observing characters. It was very much about objects that you have no emotional attachment to at all. I consider the album to be

incredibly unemotional. It's not in any way trying to pull you in. The vocals are like a grammar of noises.
Thom (2000)

It's very fragmented. Like if you walk into town one day and you pick up bits of people's lives, but only for seconds, and you don't really get any further. It's not really pursued, it's sort of just there, really. It's not a big deal, it's just happening.
Thom (2000)

This feels very different from *OK Computer*. It feels more like Bends-era in terms of our attitude on stage and where our heads are. There's just not that big cloud over our heads that we had doing *OK Computer*. There are expectations, but it's like, 'We're going to do this on our terms'.
Ed (2000)

I was completely blocked, because I couldn't sustain anything through a whole song to make it convincing, and I couldn't sustain a thought to the end of a sentence, and I couldn't sustain playing the guitar over four chords without thinking it was shit. And then eventually when the confidence came back, it came back in the form of not having a problem with that, actually using that. Saying, 'Okay, this is just fragments.' There's much more confidence than *OK Computer*.
Thom (2000)

There weren't any singles off *Kid A*, because there weren't any singles

on the record as far as we concerned. We didn't do videos because there weren't any singles. There's no great mystique to it. You just try and bluff your way through it and do what feels right. Fortunately, we've got ourselves into a position where we can do that.
Ed (2000)

We've reached the point that we can't be objective (about *Kid A*) any more because after 18 months we're too close to it. At a certain moment you have to let go and wait for the reactions of the audience. We've recorded about 20-30 songs, but we want the album to be no longer than 45 minutes. We're planning to release some of the songs that didn't make it onto the album separate and quite soon after the 'big' release.
Colin (2000)

The title just seemed to work. I think the best ones are usually like that. Often, if you call it something specific, it drives the record in a certain way. I like the non-meaning. All sorts of bizarre things have come up in relation to it. But the one I like is based on the idea that, somewhere, some errant scientist has already created the first completely genetically cloned baba – *Kid A*. I'm sure it's happened. I'm sure somewhere it's already been done, even though it's illegal now.
Thom (2000)

With us, it's never going to be a case of 'Let's tear up the blueprint and start from scratch'. When the *Kid A* reviews came out accusing of us being wilfully difficult, I was like, 'If that was true, we'd have done a much better job of it'. It's not that challenging – everything's still four minutes long, it's melodic.
Jonny (2001)

I'm not a multi-instrumentalist, so the lack of guitar worried me. Not just at the beginning but in the middle too. Even when guitars were needed, I was bereft with ideas about what to play. We all were at different times. I really hope that no album we make in future takes this long. We were working so long (during winter '99) that we didn't see daylight from one day to the next and the songs weren't coming. **Ed (2001)**
I was really, really amazed at how badly it was being viewed. People were calling it 'commercial suicide', blah-blah-blah, and saying that we were being 'intentionally difficult'. That just blew me away because the music's not that hard to grasp. We're not trying to be difficult. We're actually trying to communicate but somewhere along the line, we just seemed to piss off a lot of people.
Thom (2001)

The words themselves on *Kid A* are kind of empty because they're leaving room for the music.
Thom (2001)

I think we've been very lucky that people who are into Radiohead are willing to go with us on something. If *Kid A* came out as a début album

we'd be going off into the nether regions of obscurity by now. People who are into Radiohead have faith in what we do.
Phil (2001)

Kid A essentially needs to be listened to in one go as a 42-minute piece of music.
Ed (2001)

I expected the initial hostility to *Kid A*, as it was so different. But I am pleased that most people are saying, six months on that they now love it. We thought seriously for all of two hours about making *Kid A* and *Amnesiac* a double album. But double albums are so tough to get right, and it would have been too much for people to take in.
Ed (2001)

Not releasing a single means radio people are going to pick what they want, and the fact they picked 'Optimistic' from *Kid A* was kind of annoying.
Thom (2001)

Amnesiac

A lot of the other songs we're extremely attached to and we really like, they come from a totally different space, like socially, which is weird. They went two very different ways and you had to make choices. So we're reserving judgement on it now. I'm not sure if it'll be a complete album.
Thom (2000)

[On the title] I read that the Gnostics believe [that] when we are born we are forced to forget where we have come from in order to deal with the trauma of arriving in this life. I thought this was really fascinating. It's like the river of forgetfulness.
Thom (2001)

Amnesiac is a more straightforward set of songs than *Kid A* – each song makes sense in its own right, but I have heard other people say *Kid A* is our version of Spinal Tap's Jazz Odyssey, so I won't be surprised if the critics disagree. But for the first time, we haven't made a huge leap forward in sound from our last album. Fans who own *Kid A* should be able to get their heads around it.
Ed (2001)

It would be so easy to say *Kid A* was the experimental, dark,

brooding album, and we're coming back with the proper album one this time with all the recognisable hits. It's probably best to take both albums together and think: 'Right, this gives the full picture of what went on in those sessions'. Because there will be some pretty obtuse things on *Amnesiac* as well. We had all the recordings done for *Amnesiac* from the same sessions as *Kid A*.
Initially we thought it might be a double album, but we decided it might be a little unpalatable. It's certainly not the leftovers, and in some ways 'Amnesiac' has the stronger tracks. The tracks we selected for *Kid A* gave it an overall atmosphere and it takes a little while to translate the track and make sense of the material.
Phil (2001)

It was all finished at the same time as *Kid A*. That's why it was quite hard. We had like a board of sketches, a list of about 60 sketches – some of which were songs, others just sequences or ideas for sounds. Then it got narrowed down and narrowed down until we had a block of stuff which felt like it fitted together. And then *Kid A* pulled itself together very easily and really obviously but *Amnesiac* didn't.
Thom (2001)

There are no obvious 'here comes the chorus' moments throughout the record.
Thom (2001)

We had this whole thing about *Amnesiac* being like getting into someone's attic, opening the chest and finding their notes from a journey they'd been on. There's a story but no literal plot, so you have to keep picking out fragments. You know something really important has happened to this person that's ended up completely changing them but you're never exactly told what it is.
Thom (2001)

Our trademark was coming up for its expiry date. If we tried to carry on in that *OK Computer* vein I don't think we could have found the impetus to continue as a band. So *Kid A* and *Amnesiac* were something we needed to get out of our system. Also, doing it you recapture some of the enthusiasm in what one used to do as well. Having been together as a band for 15 years I think if we would have actually tried to carry on in the vain of *OK Computer* or *The Bends* it would have been pointless. That's never been what Radiohead is about really. It shifts. We're always changing the goalposts.
Phil (2001)

There are two frames of mind in there; a tension between our old approach of all being in a room playing together and the other extreme of manufacturing music in the studio. I think 'Amnesiac' comes out stronger in the band-arrangement way.
Phil (2001)

Album 6 – (Title unknown)

We're supposed to be going over the parts of *Amnesiac* that we haven't learnt yet. But we're just using the time to write new stuff. It's great. The songs are coming easily. It's just really nice. We've all got our confidence back.
Thom (2001)

We were rehearsing yesterday and Thom just stopped everybody and started complimenting us on what we were doing. He kept saying, 'This is really working again. It's fantastic what each of you is bringing to the piece.'
Jonny (2001)

In the studio, we got back into carefully crafting songs – the old-style sort of thing – and it was great because I found out I really missed it. I think it was from being on tour. You realise it's just kind of nice having a guitar 'round you neck, and it makes this great noise.
Thom (2001)

It's all loud and it's all guitars. It's exciting to make loud music again. It's sounding good and fresh… Loud minor chords. Distortion. Fantastic!
Thom (2001)

29

Class And Politics

You know, being a rock star is dead. It doesn't exist any more, like reading all the gossip columns about which bar they're going to. That just doesn't interest people any more, luckily. And at the same time, it's not special to be in a band any more. Anybody can do it.
Jonny (1993)

Oasis – they're a joke, aren't they? It's just lots of middle-class people applauding a bunch of guys who act stupid and write really primitive music and people say 'oh it's so honest'. It's just like the art world where they'll pick up on people outside the art world, on the periphery, and bring them in. The things they love about them are that they're out of their environment – they're working class, thick or mentally ill.
It's a freak show – they're laughing at them but at the same time they can say 'look how wonderfully varied and cultural we are'. Eventually they absorb what they were looking for and end up destroying it.
Thom (1995)

Look at the history of British bands. Most are from the middle class, with the stress on higher education. The young people turn to music as a reaction to the middle-class treadmill. They form their own little gangs.
Ed (1995)

Being in a band is about wreaking your revenge on the world. It's like when you get chucked by your first girlfriend. You just say to yourself: 'I'm going to be famous one day, and then she'll regret doing that.'
Thom (1995)

Sometimes it's confessional. Sometimes it's not. I probably felt like a creep when I wrote that song, but I don't think I'm a creep all the time. Actually, I think a lot of what we do is quite humorous, but nobody else on the planet seems to agree. Standing on a stage singing 'I want to be part of the human race'… it's got to be a bit funny, hasn't it?
Thom (1995)

I'm antagonistic rather than serious because there's so much shit around and so many people I know who are perfectly talented just don't get a chance.
Thom (1995)

We're three minutes of MTV. We're not doing anything, really. It doesn't matter how hard you try, because eventually it just gets boiled down to that. But that's okay, because at some point you meant it.
Thom (1996)

It's just that I'm surrounded by a world of grinning idiots and I don't think I want to be another one.
Thom (1996)

The middle-class thing has never been relevant. We live in Oxford, and in Oxford we're fucking lower class. The place is full of the most obnoxious, self-indulgent, self-righteous oiks on the fucking planet, and for us to be called middle class... well, no, actually. Be around on May Day when they all reel out of the pubs at five in the morning puking up and going 'haw haw haw' and trying to hassle your girlfriend...
Thom (2000)

The music scene at the moment is dominated with that terrible teenage stuff. But then other people are just getting on with it, because there's no longer that pressure to fulfil this obligation to be a rock band... Maybe that's all rubbish...
Thom (2000)

The way ad agencies work is to suck the blood of any vaguely original or unique thing in order to breathe life into their dead creations. We expend too much effort creating this stuff to have someone appropriate it for whatever junk they're trying to flog.
Thom (2001)

I think the Nineties are great musically but politically they're fucking frightening.
Thom (1995)

I hope we don't speak for anyone. I do think we were brought up under the Reagan-Thatcher administrations, when the attitude was 'Go out and get what you want.' I think that environment has produced a very disaffected youth. Even I, who love and believe in politics, feel a great sense of futility. In the United States, for example, it seems as though the government would continue to run without the two parties. The system doesn't give people a real choice.
Ed (1995)

Britain's just been completely fucked over by the Tories, and I think that bands haven't wanted to write about it because there's nothing you can do about it. Music's just become escapism, and I can't really stomach it any longer. I want to try to redress that balance in the stuff we're writing now. I don't know how I'm going to do it, but it seems to be the only thing worth doing right now.
Thom (1996)

For three hours when the Labour Party got in, people were nice to each other. That was it. It's been bullshit ever since. I didn't watch it happening. It was so obvious they were going to win. I won't be going to 10 Downing Street, put it that way.
Thom (1998)

We need to change our economic relationship with the rest of the world from the master/slave to something similar to democracy... I think it's very much the West's fault. I think this is all a legacy of the Cold War. Putting in place brutal and corrupt regimes to try and maintain a covert hold over large areas of the

Third World. I think everyone should be worried because people are dying because of it.
Thom (1999), on his involvement with Drop The Debt.

I spent the first few years of being in Radiohead not aware of outside issues like these. I had tunnel vision, but as we travelled a lot it became very obvious that the wonderful West was not the wonderful West we thought it was... the trip to Mexico and Thailand made that bloody obvious. My personal experience was in some way feeling that everyone was trying to be Western but it was obvious that the countries were only doing this because culturally they had been destroyed and they were at the West's mercy.
Thom (1999)

I'm a champagne socialist, apparently. Someone called me that last night. I got into a massive row with this guy. Personally, I was happy to get involved in Jubilee 2000, the Drop The Debt thing, because it's a mainstream, acceptable face of the resistance against the antics of the IMF and the World Bank. But equally, I'm interested in the unacceptable face of it, the disruptive elements, the anarchists, because I don't really care what methods are used to make the IMF and World Bank so incredibly unpopular that they dismantle it. I don't really care how it happens, as long as it happens. That's the point.
Thom (2000)

I'm in no way proud to be British at all, really. I'm just not interested in the place. When Blair first came to power I got heavily involved in reading all about what was going on, about his 'third way' and how he was going to develop a relationship with business which was going to be of benefit to this country. That obviously was never going to work. And it didn't.
Thom (2001)

I went down to Sinai and then I stayed in Eilat for a while. I've met wonderful people, Arabs and Jews. I've never encountered such hospitality and generosity. They weren't even nice to me because I was in a famous band, but just because I sat down with them to drink coffee and chat. It got me thinking that it's amazing how people that couldn't stand each other are capable of such goodness and generosity. It's very frustrating. But that's the history of the human race – you can meet wonderful people on both sides, but they'll do horrible things to each other.
Ed (2001)

The really important issues in politics are the Third World debt and the relationship between the First World and the Third World, and trade laws… None of this stuff is ever discussed as a political issue. It's all in the realm of the economists and that is fucked up.
Thom (2001)

Hard Pressed

It's always been kind of muted, the music press to us, until very recently. They're kind of suddenly coming around. It's like when we brought 'Creep' out, it received a fairly indifferent review in *New Musical Express*. And then four months later, they were describing it as a classic single, as if they'd finally come around to liking it. It's very strange.
Jonny (1993)

There's very much the British feeling of 'I'm not worthy, why am I here?'. Certainly, there's an implicit neurosis about how the press is going to treat you... And when we signed with our record company there were a lot of weird political things going on. It's learning to actually isolate yourself from relying on people around you. I'm kind of a kid about things like that. It stresses me out. I'd like to go back and play with my building blocks and just let my parents worry about the record.
Thom (1993)

We had a live following here (in the US), but the music press hated us because we were signed with EMI, a major. We've never been considered *NME* or *Melody Maker* cover material because of it. When we first released 'Creep' in Britain (in September 1992), an *NME* journalist said to me, 'If you weren't on EMI, you'd have had a cover by now.' In America, they don't have

that kind of snobbishness about major labels.
Ed (1994)

I stopped reading the press when they printed I was going to top myself. And my girlfriend rings me up really, really upset, saying, 'What's all this, what have you been saying?' You know, that's when I stopped reading it. That was enough for me... I'm in this business, but I also want to be in this business on my own terms.
Thom (1995)

It seemed that while we were this little band out on the edges making our music, no one had any grudges. But as soon as 'Creep' hit, everyone got out their knives and came running.
Colin (1995)

Some of the things they said smarted. We're very close knit and every member takes the criticism personally. About the worst thing they said was that not only was Radiohead a one-hit wonder but the band would never evolve past the sound of 'Creep'. If you listen to *Pablo Honey* with an open mind, you'll see that 'Creep' isn't representative of the direction of the band. It sticks out from the others.
Colin (1995)

I thought that basically it was the British press that did it to Richey

(Edwards of Manic Street Preachers). Full stop. Although I've got lots of friends who are journalists, the few who I think were basically responsible for him having a breakdown I will always hold responsible and I will always see what we do in that light… And I think he is still alive.
Thom (1995)

I'm not very good at dealing with day-to-day press interviews, as most people in my position aren't, because they get very precious about the way people think about them. I'm not that precious about the way people think about me, but I am precious about offensive stuff that people write – and I am precious about headlines like the one that was put in the *NME*, 'Thom's Temper Tantrum'.
Thom (1995)

The *New Musical Express* said I stormed off in a tantrum rather than I'd lost my voice. The headline was 'Thommy's Temper Tantrum'. They just wanted to use the alliteration. It's so vacant, so begrudging – I can't deal with that level of malice aimed at me personally. I'd be paralysed by hate. I just can't read it. It's what journalists have dreamt up over their glass of lager in the afternoon.
Thom (1996)

A few people write in specific magazines that are really influential, and everyone just reiterates it again and again and again. And whatever the sentiment was in the original review turns into this garbled echo, which really winds me up.
Thom (1998)

For selfish reasons I'm quite happy to see Thom on the cover of magazines – that's only because it means we get bothered less.
Jonny (1998)

It's not like we make people sign contracts, like a lot of American bands do. I don't think we've ever told people what they can and can't ask.
Ed (2000)

Even if we appeared on *The Muppet Show* they'd still say we're dark figures. Okay, the truth is that there are some things you just can't change. However, I find it very difficult to express our feelings about these songs because we still feel very attached to them, so we can't be objective about them.
Phil (2000)

The thing I have a problem with is the fact that so much of what people – of what journalists – term rock music now is really not based on the music itself, but based on the lifestyle that goes with it. It's like a lifestyle choice… That doesn't mean that people should stop using drums and guitars, but why stand up and say, 'I'm a rock star – in 10 years time I'm going to get fucked up on smack…' The mythology around it has run its course and is stale and uncreative now, and it has been destroying the people who've been trying to make the music.
Thom (2000)

We started doing this thing every Thursday, these webcasts… It's called Amateur Night, it's very unprofessional in a way, but it's honest, it's true. Because it's us. And the website is us. It's not the record company. We own everything.
Colin (2000)

I don't read interviews but I always read reviews. A lot of people obviously just hadn't heard it (*Kid A*) enough, and they just wanted to be first out of the box. It was that thing where one person writes a bad review and then the floodgates open. In the US, we got these amazing reviews, but I think that was just because people had had the record for longer.
Ed (2000)

I think, as long as you keep moving, you're all right. The thing is you're always developing and expanding. It's a protean thing and a public image can't keep pace with it. So it – the process of success – is like this slow-drying glue that sets around you, that slows you down and gums you up. And while all that's happening, your own life's going on at the side of it, with your own relationships and your own experiences and that becomes sort of calcified as well. And the whole thing just grinds to a halt really. And then you suddenly find yourself in the paper or on the cover of a magazine and your life and experiences have become summarised. And once it's summarised, its over. So the trick is to try to be in the corner of people's vision, but not full on.
Colin (2000)

I think you have a duty to let people know what you're up to and communicate with them if you expect them to have any interest in your music.
Jonny (2000)

On 'Life In A Glasshouse' (on *Amnesiac*) I'm desperate for people to understand all the words because they're really important. It began after I read this interview with the wife of a very famous actor who the tabloids completely hounded for three months… She got the copies of the papers with her picture and she pasted them up all over the house, over all the windows so that all the cameras that were outside on her lawn only had their own images to photograph.
I thought that was brilliant, and that's where the song started from… I just thought 'Nobody deserves this'. Especially when they're a completely innocent party. From there, it developed into a complete rant about tabloid journalism destroying people at will, tying people to the stake and watching them burn – an activity that seems to be particularly rife in this country.
Thom (2001)

We weren't playing the magazine game properly. We just felt at the time, 'We've earned a licence to do this. Let's just do it.' But the media responded by suddenly thinking, 'Oh, so they're not going to play ball. We're going to go after them.' I just felt, 'What the hell's going on?' We're only making music here. Come on.
Thom (2001)

No one's being compared to us any more because of our collective acts of commercial suicide.
Colin (2001)
We were primed for a lynching (after *Kid A*). It was damned no matter what, really. And then I guess we sort of fucked up because people were only allowed to hear the record

once and then were forced to write a review. So all the reviewers were saying, 'Uh, this isn't Radiohead, we don't recognise it, it might be good later on, but right now I don't get it all'.
Thom (2001)

It is rubbish when bands don't do interviews, but we do them and we do them really badly. It's like, why bother? I think we lack the media training to not be confused and contradictory, so who knows?
Jonny (2001)

We don't hate the media, it's just that when there's too much of it we get bored, but it happens to every human being. I don't think we even hated the media by the time that movie (*Meeting People Is Easy*) was made. We were just tired.
Ed (2001)

R.E.M.

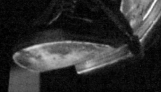

Heroes, Influences And Contemporaries

I met Stone Gossard (of Pearl Jam). I had Neil Young standing behind me while we were playing, which was a bit unnerving. And they're fans of our record. It was great. **Colin (1995)**

I wanted to meet R.E.M. and Elvis Costello and now I have.
Thom (1995)

We got wind of the fact that R.E.M. was going to invite us on the tour. What do you think, either four weeks on our own, playing in clubs of 600 people, or with the biggest band in the world, who you're massive fans of? There's not really any question of what you're going to do. We'd have walked across America for three days and not eaten anything or drunk anything to do this tour.
Ed (1995)

Everything that we've come to expect was turned completely on its head, like the idea that you get to a certain level and you lose it and that's it – you're lost – and for everything to be amicable and there be no bitchiness or pettiness about it. On stage R.E.M. were playing songs they've written, mucking around with the idea of being who they are and having no illusions about it – or seemingly so. And you compare that with a lot of what we feel when we are at home and it was just so different. It's just such a headfuck.
Thom (1995)

If someone had told me this time last summer that we'd be touring with R.E.M. we'd probably tell them where to go. The likelihood of it was so small. So we've been very lucky. It's also been a very good introduction to the world of bigger stages and bigger audiences and the difficulties of playing such personal music on such a public footing.
Jonny (1995)

Shit Shit Shit, this is R.E.M. and they really like us. No, I mean they REALLY like us, they're not just being nice. When someone you really admire gives you something like that, your shoulders get a little lighter, you feel a little stronger, forever.
Thom (1995)

It was a big relief to find them (R.E.M.) so keyed up and writing new songs all the time... still finding passion in what they're doing. I thought they'd be less enthusiastic after touring so much. But it was the opposite. They were so fired up and so into the music that it was encouraging.
Jonny (1996)

What REM gave us was a sense that you can be as emotional as you like in what you do. That's what it's about. It was extraordinarily good therapy.
Thom (1996)

Pink Floyd has been a new discovery for me, it's only been a year or so since I started listening to them. Traditionally Pink Floyd were terrible, everybody liked them at

but there's basically good forms of everything. Like country and western I once decided was all terrible, and then I found these early songs from the Forties and Fifties that are basically all about cocaine and women and people dying and very grim and hard-core, and some of the music is great. So, I'm happy to be proved wrong.
Jonny (1998)

Left to right: Bono, Bjork, Talking Heads, Elvis Costello, Scott Walker and Michael Stipe

school, they were always extremely boring people. The only record I remember coming out was *The Wall*, which I hated, and don't really like now either. But then I discovered all the early Pink Floyd and I was very impressed. Some of it's great.
Jonny (1998)

I'm just prepared to accept that there's good music in everything, except possibly, march band music,

They all think we're going to be the next stadium band. Take U2 and R.E.M.'s baton. If it happens, it happens, but the only way it will happen is if we're comfortable with that… which we're not at the moment. And as long as the show's not compromised. I know it's possible to do amazing shows: I saw the U2 'PopMart' thing. There's no way you could do that inside – it's phenomenal. It was very moving, it was very personal at

times, and it was extravagant and over the top. And it was fantastic. That's the way to do those things.
Ed (1998)

I'm good at writing with eras of music and then discovering that I love whole hoards of it. Like I always found a lot of dub reggae, I didn't really like it, then I got some Horace Andy – *Scientist Meets Space Invaders* is another amazing

Coltrane, people who we are equally stealing from. The difference is that they're not in fashion or aren't perceived as so cutting edge. No-one sat down and said, 'How can you so shamelessly take the texture of Alice Coltrane's second album and put it on one of your songs?'
Jonny (2000)

album – and found myself trying to copy sounds from that kind of record. I had similar things with people like Olivier Messiaen and Scott Walker. Miles Davis has been a big influence on (*OK Computer*), *Bitches Brew* especially. We are happy to steal anything from anywhere really.
Jonny (1998)

We should also be getting a kicking for ripping off Mingus and Alice

When I did the session with Björk (for the track 'I've Seen It All' from Selma Songs), she had all the same records. It was great, actually. But coming from being in a rock band, I had no confidence in exploring that stuff. I felt I knew nothing about it so I didn't have the right to go into it. There was all this baggage. Rock bands going into making electronic music have a fairly bad history, Neil Young being an obvious example.
Thom (2000)

Bowie, in the Seventies, was a reference, and it is to that we aspire. He did not stop composing, he changed his style continuously… We would like to release many more CDs. Of course, in this case, it is possible that you can release a bad CD, but you continue to evolve, you test things. Bowie is a musician, but he works like a painter. Thom always thought we should aspire to that.
Ed (2000)

each other. On the later Beatles albums, when they got really, really good at putting things next to each other, like on *The White Album*, it's just amazing. How in the hell can you have three different versions of 'Revolution' on the same record and get away with it?
Thom (2000)

I was much more into the electronica stuff like Autechre and Aphex Twin, lots of stuff on the

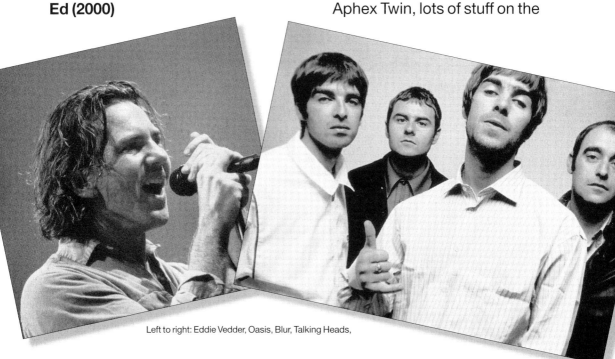

Left to right: Eddie Vedder, Oasis, Blur, Talking Heads,

We thought about making two CDs, 45 minutes each… but the songs need to breathe. Look at *What's Going On* by Marvin Gaye: 43 marvellous minutes… Proposing a long album is like eating too much. However excellent the food, there is a time you want to stop, you're fed up and want to take a break.
Ed (2000)

You can put all the best songs in the world on a record and they'll ruin

Warp label. I always regretted that we, in deciding being a rock band and touring ourselves stupid and turning into little monsters, we lost the chance of ever being able to get into that sort of music and that was a big regret for me 'cause I didn't see it as any different from rock music, from where I sat. If it's good, it's good. It's got the same 'Fuck Me' attitude if it's good.
Thom (2000)

We all are really heavily obsessed by *Remain In Light*, the Talking Heads' album, the way they did that and the sort of emotions that go with that record…

When David Byrne was writing the lyrics for that record he had notes, no songs. Start a rhythm, here's a riff and it keeps going. What I admire about *Remain In Light* is that everything is essentially fragments 'cause he's taking things from notebooks. So what I often

records as good as Al Green.
Ed (2001)

When Oasis and Blur were having their battle it felt like Radiohead were on the sidelines, holding everyone's coat. Then when we released *OK Computer*, it was like we gave them their coats back, all patched up. I loved Blur's 'Parklife', and Oasis's first two records were amazing, but that battle they waged was depressing and belittling to

tried to do with the writer's block thing was basically stopped throwing away all the things that didn't work, which I was doing before, and keeping them and cutting them up and throwing them all in a top hat and pulling them out.
Thom (2000)

We always felt this massive affinity with them (Talking Heads) because they were white folks grooving in a 'college geeky' way and still making

both parties. Both groups were too naïve; they were functioning at a primary-school level of media manipulation.
Colin (2001)

I did stop listening to 'bands' almost completely, though. If I needed to feel better about music I'd listen to Mingus. I also really liked (Aphex Twin) Richard D James' album. There was a tape of Bud Powell, the jazz pianist – that I subsequently

lost – that I played for a lot of inspiration.
Thom (2001)

We finally met Scott Walker at the Meltdown festival. He's a top geezer – a really nice bloke. We did that gig for him basically. I was on-stage the whole time thinking, 'Scott Walker's in the audience. I don't give a shit who else is here.'
Thom (2001)

People distrust learning, don't they? There's all these stories of Miles Davis going to the Juilliard Academy and poring over classical scores in the library. That side of Miles is glossed over a bit in favour of the living-on-the-edge stuff. But it just makes me love him even more, the idea of him wanting to get musical inspiration from everything and everywhere.
Jonny (2001)

I like Low at the moment, their new LP – *Things We Lost In The Fire*.
Thom (2001)

Art Blakey's just insane. If you can get an Art Blakey album and put it on, and you can hear, every four seconds there'll be a break that will have informed a whole vein of contemporary hip-hop. He's just insane with his drum breaks and old-school hip-hop drum beats within the concept of a drum kit and percussion.
All those people we talk about, we cite them as producing an inspirational collection of sound and arrangement ideas, lying to

ourselves in terms of our technical virtuosity, 'cause there's obviously no way that we could ever be like any of those people, but the way that those people select, edit and present their music is what inspires us.
Colin (2001)

With Outkast, we really like their music and we enjoy their wide musical ambition and sweep and the fact that people who we respect should like us as well – as part of another world and culture – is really exciting, you know?
Colin (2001)

When you've been on stage with Johnny Marr and Eddie Vedder it's quite a humbling experience really. It is very bizarre. It's like watching your record collection performing in front of you and then behind it, actually part of it. You always feel as though you're playing catch-up with people like that.
Phil (2001)

I think we've all been envious about the way Björk has been able to reinvent music. Also, I've been influenced by Aphex Twin, Boards of Canada, and Autechre. They truly seem to be the pioneers of new sound at the moment. While the band format is still valid, the really exciting things going on in music now are created in people's bedrooms.
Ed (2001)

Playing with Neil (Finn) has been a real apprenticeship and an eye opener. We're going home with lots of ideas to work on. There's a real lesson for us coming out here (to New Zealand).
Phil (2001)

Neil (Finn) is the most prolific writer of great songs.
Ed (2001)

Neil Finn

Image And Fame

(Pop stardom) lives up to what I'd imagined and more. It's like joining the circus or something.
Thom (1993)

It's frightening. We still feel very much like a new band, really. It just feels very fast.
Jonny (1993)

We had knickers thrown at us in Detroit – we left 'em to the guitar technicians – and girls were in the front row, screaming 'We love you!' It was really strange.
Ed (1994)

You go from being a band that's pretty inconsequential on EMI's worldwide roster to being a priority up there alongside Pink Floyd.
Thom (1995)

It's pretty difficult not to love the attention. And I went through a phase of going to London a lot and going to parties and things. Part of me really wanted to do that, wanted to go out and sort of soak up this beaming fucking sunshine coming out of my bottom or whatever it was, but you know… Maybe I should have done it, but it's not my thing, that's all. I'm not good at taking compliments, but I do it. I think it's more that people have put this level of significance into it, to the point where it's really taking the piss.
Thom (1995)

We definitely suffered from that British disease of being reserved. But playing live gave us that chance to shake off the shackles and the chains.
Ed (1995)

The whole thing about 'Creep' was it upset our plans. We'd always planned to have this evolution, and then by the fifth album maybe we'd have a gold record. We had a gold record on the first album – that was a bit of a shock. If you'd asked us that beforehand, we wouldn't have wanted it that way. It made the expectations a lot bigger than we wanted, and it wasn't necessarily fair.
Ed (1995)

That's not to say the album's a sham I've been through some really bad times, and I wrote about them but I hate these self-pitying rock stars who run headlong into situations that damage them, and then whine about it. I've no sympathy. It's so easy to be miserable. Being happy is tougher and cooler.
Thom (1995)

What Stipe does is immerse himself in it. He reads everything that's written about them. Which is what I used to do. But I found there was so much bad I couldn't read it. I had to stop reading all of it. Personally I've had things written about me that

have really, really hurt. It's not actually that nice to be called ugly more than 10 times in a year in the press. I didn't get into this fucking business because I was beautiful.
Thom (1995)

We don't think we're special now or anything. We're not into the whole groupie thing. For us the most important thing is to put on a good show.
Ed (1995)

That whole idea of being Thom Yorke the personality… I don't want to die having been just that. The whole thing that most pop stars are desperately trying to attain immortality is through the cult of their personality… this phenomenon, this Sunday review section, glossy front page… It's like 'NO!, actually. I don't want to be remembered for this, I want to be remembered for doing pieces of work that people liked, and other than that I don't really want to know.' I'm not into this for immortality's sake. Sixty years from now, I'm going to be dead, and that will be that.
Thom (1995)

My father asked the other day how it was going and I said, 'Oh you know, it could be better from our point of view'. It's similar to when someone suffers from bulimia and looks in the mirror and thinks they're too fat when they're really thin. We're getting this amazing response from people and we're thinking it isn't good enough.
Ed (1995)

I think the more we are doing and the more successful we are being, the harder it is to deal with on a personal level and to connect with personal wants and needs and personal life. You understand why people get caught up with quick fixes like drugs because it is quite a numbing experience. I was thinking about Blind Melon with *No Rain*: they had already toured that album at least twice before it was a success and they had to tour it again. And you can go mad. It's bizarre, it's like being in a band is a privileged, rarefied existence and you should never get complacent about it but at the same time there are pressures about it.
Colin (1995)

I suppose it's quite funny, that idea of everything that you do, 24 hours a day, that when you go and have breakfast or go out into the street, that every single minute of every single day you're conscious of the fact that people might be watching you, is really, really unhealthy. The whole cult of personality surrounding bands, I think, is pointless. And I think the Eighties really bore that out.
Obviously people want to know about the people that make the music, but by the end of it, it was just becoming so pompous. Like with the whole U2 thing at the end of Eighties, and like Madonna and so on, it all became an extension of the whole Saatchi and Saatchi concept that you can sell anything to anybody if you put it across the right way.
Thom (1995)

I get people coming up on the streets in Oxford saying, 'Can I have your autograph?' Sometimes I'll say 'Yes' and sometimes I'll be really, really rude because they'll catch me when I'm not being Thom Yorke from Radiohead, like in a restaurant or something and it'll be, 'No, piss off'. But then to have people come back and say, 'We heard you're a bit difficult, a bit weird, you're not very easy to talk to'. It's the circumstance that people are talking to you in, when people come up and they want a little bit of you, their two cents' worth.

And that, to be perfectly honest, is not why I got into this…

You feel like saying to them 'Look, this is not why I got into this, and I don't really give a flying fuck whether you have my autograph or not and I'd rather you didn't bother me because if I was anyone else in the street you wouldn't.

Thom (1995)

I do get into a panic. I get really nervous that I'm not weird enough. And then I think, 'Hang on. This is completely ridiculous. What's the point of that?' There are groups that expend so much time and energy proving how larger-than-life they are. For who? For whose benefit? If you're going to do it, prove it in your music and shut up.
Thom (1996)

I think, if this doesn't sound too corporate, that Radiohead is a big badge to hide behind. Radiohead is something that we push forward instead of ourselves… And also I sometimes feel like there's a sixth member of the band sitting listening to what we're doing, and every time we've done something he shouts, 'Bored now!'.
Jonny (2000)

If you send out signals that you're not interested in the conventional trappings of the world you inhabit, people don't intrude on you.
Colin (2000)

I'm fed up of seeing my face everywhere. It got to the point where I didn't feel like I owned it. We're not interested in being celebrities, and others seem to have different plans for us.
Thom (2000)

We happen to live in an age where recorded music is distributed throughout the world and bands are held up to be almost superhuman. It's not a very healthy thing.
Ed (2000)

We'd really like to have more regular communications with people, as opposed to just having this massive dump every two-and-a-half years, and fanfares and clarion calls.
Colin (2000)

It feels like Radiohead are famous. But that no one knows who we are. Which is brilliant, really.
Jonny (2000)

Bono's a very positive guy and he recognises that to be in the arena that U2 are in, you have to put up with a lot of crap so that his music can get on the radio and spread a feeling of general well-being everywhere it's played. The thing about Thom – and this extends to all of us – is that we just don't think it's worth it. To get to that stage, you have to go through so much crap. And along the way, you're bound to fall prey to the system. They'll get you somehow. We kind of dipped into that situation with *OK Computer*… you come out at the end and you're half a person.
Ed (2001)

In a way the spotlight was off us and we were able to develop at a more natural rate. It doesn't do any band any favours having that hype at an early stage. We've always been very uneasy with this rock band tag. I think there's a bit more to us than a rock band. But, in the sense that we go out touring as a rock band I suppose we are. It's one of those terms you can be uncomfortable with because it can be quite
Phil (2001)

To be honest, when (audience adulation) first starts happening, the novelty of it is just amazing. But it gets problematic when it becomes habit-forming, like when you're Aerosmith or something. If you let 50,000 people into your brain every day, then you're going to have trouble ushering them out.
Thom (2001)

It's like having an appointment at Savile Row to have a suit fitted. You don't turn up but still they end up cutting you this huge flamboyant outfit that Bono wore previously and which he passed on to Michael Stipe. Then you finally turn up and collect a pair of pyjamas instead.
Colin (2001)

I tell you what's really ridiculous – going into a bookshop and there's all these books about yourself. In a way, it feels like you're already dead. So you've got a license to start again.
Thom (2001)

53

Insider Dealings And Feelings

Years and years of tension and not saying anything to each other, and basically all the things that had built up since we'd met each other all came out in one day. We were spitting and fighting and crying and saying all the things that you don't want to talk about, and I think if we hadn't ever done that... I think that completely changed what we did and we all went back and did the album (*The Bends*) and it all made sense.
Thom (1995)

It was that typical Radiohead thing, things had been brewing. We're not really confrontational with one another. Things had been brewing and they basically came to a head. We were all completely knackered on this Mexican tour bus, 12 of us, with six bunks and they were about 5 feet 6 inches long, so you're getting no sleep. It was just ridiculous. It was something we'd been spending eight or nine years working towards and it was like, we'd never been totally honest with each other in terms of... We're not into bonding, we're friends and everything, but because of maybe our upbringing or the school that we went to we don't tell each other our problems. We deal with them ourselves. It's the only way you can deal with them.
Ed (1995)

The biggest change it's made in my life is a sad one. We've gone from being a bunch of friends in a band which wasn't the be-all and end-all of their lives to being a pop success, with all the lifestyle elements that come attached. It's very easy to get used to good fortune, even as you're aware of the capriciousness of it. It's scary to realise this Radiohead thing has taken over my life.
Jonny (1995)

We'd just finished doing a tour in Britain that hadn't gone very well, and we were feeling as low as we'd felt since we started – it would have been more useful to make the next record because there seemed nothing else to do. And then 'Creep' started taking off. It was frustrating, being judged on just that song when we felt we needed to move on. We were forced on tour to support it, and it gagged us, really.
We were on the verge of breaking up. It was a lesson. The way that modern music culture works is that bands get set in a period of time, and then they repeat that small moment of their lives for evermore – that's what everybody wants. And that's just what we weren't going to do.
Thom (1995)

Probably our biggest criticism of ourselves is we think too much.

We all went to university and have never thought there was anything wrong with thinking too much.
Ed (1995)

I think we're learning not to think too much about stuff. Thought can be an inhibiting thing. I don't know if you've read Arthur Miller's autobiography *Time Bends*, but analysis can be crippling thing and self-consciousness can be a crippling thing – but it can also be a source of great creativity, and articulation of crises of thought can be a great thing in itself.
Colin (1995)

I don't know if anybody else has this feeling. When you're walking down the street and you catch your reflection in something like a car window or a shop window and you see your face and you think, 'Who's that?'
Thom (1995)

At the moment I'm really excited about what we could do, but just as much, like 50 per cent of the time, I'm thinking how close it is to being completely banal. I guess that's what's supposed to happen.
Thom (1995)

Call us 'sick pop'. Well, maybe a little bit melancholy, but with pop overtures and sensibilities.
Ed (1995)

I spend 99 per cent of my time worrying about what it is we're doing. For someone else to actually feel it's in any way inspiring to them… I just can't get my head around that. It's amazing how much confidence completely changes a band.
Thom (1996)

We were hysterical. One moment we'd be giggling, the next we'd be really down. Our reactions were extreme.
Ed (1997)

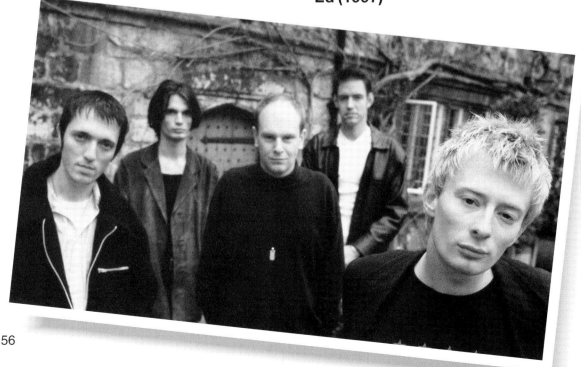

I'm disappointed by almost everything I hear, but at the same time, I feel like I'm fluking… We're holding each other up. There are no budding solo artists in this band. **Jonny (1998)**

I think we play pretty well as a band now. Am I stretched by being in the band? Yeah, I think everyone is. There was a very good article written about us which said, 'They're musically adventurous, but they don't get pompous or hark back to prog rock, because the punk thing is still in there.' That's very true. We're all learning.
Ed (1998)

We learned to be human beings again, rather than monsters. And that translated to how we worked. I mean, I'm probably never going

to be the easiest person in the studio because I get frustrated. I can hear something in my head, and it's not happening. There's only so much patience you can have. This fragmented way has made that easier, because I'm not trying to sustain one grand emotion. And having a lack of attachment to what I'm writing doesn't make the work any less powerful.
Thom (2000)

It kinda sends you back to a place, it makes you feel ill. Once you finished the record it's like you have all this power and emotion of doing it, as you're doing it, and when it's finished, it's over, that's it. It's very difficult then to be able to connect with it. It's other people's, it's other people's property. And that's a good thing, that's how it's supposed to be.
Thom (2000)

I think the turmoil that is required is one that you can find any day walking down the street. I don't think you need to go and seek it out. Any normal human being goes through states of flux which they need to resolve by talking to people, making their art or whatever.
Thom (2000)

I still find you can get excited when you look in people's eyes when they walk down the street and sometimes you see really nasty, terrifying things. But most of the time you just see a bunch of people trying to get it together and there's something really hopeful in that. It sounds a bit bonkers, but there you go.
Thom (2000)

I got really into these hawthorn hedges in the woods near where I live. The way the branches weave together reminds me of a human brain and I love the way that the rain flows along them and the life that's lived in them – it's like this path you choose to take and it gets thinner at the end. And I used to draw these things endlessly, for weeks on end, I used to go sit in the woods and draw these trees. I still do it.
Thom (2000)

It was really because I had felt that I totally lost control of any element of my life, of anything I was involved in. And ultimately being so incredibly angry it was inexpressible. When we finished the record I realised that this was what it was all about.
Thom (2000)

In terms of the relationship between the five of us, everything was up for grabs last year. It was a case of trying to see what different musical approaches there were – whether they were appropriate, whether we were prepared to do them and whether we could find something we all agreed on.
Phil (2000)

We discovered there are certain tasks that you have to do on your own, but basically, the best stuff comes out of collaboration with other people. It's all happening at the same time. In our studio we have everything set up in different areas of the same space…
Thom (2000)

New Year's Eve '98 was one of the lowest points in my life. I felt I was going fucking crazy. Every time I picked up a guitar I just got the horrors. I would start writing a song, stop after 16 bars, hide it away in a drawer, look at it again, tear it up, destroy it… I was sinking down and down.
Thom (2000)

I always used to use music as a way of moving on and dealing with things and I felt the thing that helped me deal with things had been sold to the highest bidder and I was simply doing its bidding. I couldn't handle that. And that was all sort of wrapped up with feeling huge amounts of guilt about something that, when it was good, just came naturally anyway. So it all just went round and round in

circles for ages. So there's no bravado about 'We're gonna shake this shit up', really. It's more like, 'I can't carry on like this.'
Thom (2000)

It's like being trapped in one space, on one point. And you can't go backwards and you can't go forwards, you can't go in any direction. You're absolutely trapped in one particularly space in time and you cannot move on. And I use music to move on, to progress through life. So when I lost that, I lost the ability to progress, so you lose the ability to interact and it becomes a vicious circle.
Thom (2000)

Every time you do some music or read a book or go for a drive in your car you're constantly thinking you're trapped. You're stuck, you're on a full stop. There'll never be anything else. I think the only way you'll deal with it eventually is just forget about it. You choose to not have a problem with it, you choose to go and see your friends, go out and get drunk with them, enjoy life, forget about it, waiting for it to come back.
Thom (2000)

It's interesting that a lot of people this year have decided that there's some kind of masterplan to what we do. They think we're stuck away in the heart of the Oxford countryside plotting and scheming, and the reality of it is that a lot of what we do happens by chance.
Ed (2000)

Just going a certain way for a long, long time, and not being able to stop or look back or consider where I was. For, like, 10 years. Not being able to connect with anything. Becoming completely unhinged, in the best sense of the word. **Thom (2000)**

I think there's a lot of not really trusting anybody in being lost. I didn't trust people at all, not even the people closest to me for ages and ages, and that means you really have nothing to hold on to. 'Everything In Its Right Place' is about that. You're trying to fit into the right place and the right box so you can connect. **Thom (2000)**

I find it very destabilising to constantly have to work with different people. It's good to have security around you. I need it. **Thom (2001)**

It's a pretty shit turnout… something like two minutes of music a month. However, personally speaking, a lot of other shit needed to be sorted out, which was nobody's business but ours. We couldn't stay in the same place… The alternative was nothing again ever, if you know what I mean. **Thom (2001)**

I think I've started to accept that there are cyclical peaks and troughs to what we do. Of course, now the worry is things will become too much of a cycle – in the past year so much has happened now I'm worried that we'll get really complacent. **Thom (2001)**

On the last two records, people felt that Thom's concerns were inarticulate for various reasons, whether they felt they didn't have a voice or they, uh, just whether it was just himself or other people he was writing about in the songs. There's feelings of powerlessness and that kind of stuff and those ideas are of interest, things like Naomi Klein's (book) *No Logo*, concepts of intrusion by corporations into personal space and things like that. **Colin (2001)**

The personal crap is gone, which basically, I think, was the product of being put in a weird place after *OK Computer*. In order to evolve you can't let the lifestyle – which is a horrendous word that I hate – take over. You can't let the life you choose to lead take over from the reason you got to lead that life in the first place. And the culture surrounding the rock business is itself a kind of self-fulfilling prophecy. Which is why I get so jealous of artists who are able to just issue 12-inchers and never really get involved in the press but still get their music to people. But in actual fact, I've discovered coming back to this stuff after three years that I like bits of it. I've found I actually like having to explain myself. **Thom (2001)**

We did talk at one time about doing certain things under our name and certain things under a different name, because it seemed to make things easier. But I've always been

massively 'anti' that because what you're doing then is just a bunch of compartmentalising bollocks. It's putting music into pointless little boxes and pretending it should be viewed in different ways. Why not put it all out under the same name?
Thom (2001)

There were lots of depressingly frank exchanges of opinion late into the night. But the sad thing about it is that very few of our arguments were to do with the music: it was just 'fall out'… Personally speaking, during that time I was a total fuckin' mess. No one could say anything to me without me turning round and launching a vicious tirade at them.
Thom (2001)

All I was since leaving college was in this band. That's all I did. And everything else was utterly irrelevant or else just a pain in the arse. To the point where I sort of lost the connection with everything and ended up driving myself a bit round the bend.
Thom (2001)

Too fucking middle class, that's our problem!
Thom (2001)

At one point, I started to believe that if you sit down and analyse what you're doing, worry about it, then you're not being your true self. But, for instance, [The Fall's] Mark E Smith is not a noble savage – he's a fucking intellectual. With us, though, there's this suspicion of calculation all the way through what we do. Where does this come from, the idea that if you sit down and think about something you can't be emotional in any way? Maybe it's some sort of punk hang-up. Sometimes, I think they're right about us. Sometimes we do over-think things.
Thom (2001)

The reason people are so into escaping is there's a fucking lot to escape from. In a way, the last thing anyone needs is someone rubbing salt in the wounds, which is sort of what we're doing.
Thom (2001)

A tortured soul is a tortured soul and will eventually cease to function in any useful way unless they get help. Unless they sail to the land of happy every now and again, where everything is the right way up, then they will simply fall off the edge of the world. A good way I've found to navigate is with songs and music. But there is a trade-off somewhere; at least there seems to be for the people I know.
Thom (2001)

Beats Instrumental

I like to work with a desk where, even though I'm not personally engineering, I know what every knob is doing. We used a Trident which is like an old Seventies desk, when we were mixing the album, and I liked that because it was so simple – even I understood what was going on, and I'm not an engineer.
Thom (1993)

For some people drumming is like a sport. I try to work on technique in order to open my powers of expression. It's just being scared of making mistakes; it's concentrating!
Phil (1996)

I'm just not that in love with the guitar or anything else, really. I've yet to find an instrument that has really obsessed me. I'm happy to skip around from glockenspiel to whatever else the song needs.
Jonny (1998)

It's not very hard to reproduce what we do on records, because there are so many of us and there are so many instruments lying around the stage. Also we are all quite prepared to do nothing for half a song. We all realise that if we are needed for ten seconds in the middle of one song, and that's all, then that's what we do. Nobody complains.
Jonny (1998)

With all the technology and software now available, you can take things and manipulate them in ways that you've never been able to do before. That's definitely something we're going to get more and more into; taking guitars and cutting them up, making sounds that have never been made... Everything is wide open with technology now. The permutations are endless.
Ed (2000)

Thom's lyrics are more fragmented. Some of the vocals are buried in music, but there will also be some very powerful singing as one might expect from him. We have tried new technologies, new sounds, new effects. In-between the songs there are electronic, ambient intermezzos.
Colin (2000)

(*Kid A*) was created by a computer program that Thom wrote and we all built a song on it by using electronic organs and different sounds. It is undoubtedly characteristic of the new ways we use to write songs, and we are still experimenting with new sounds.
Phil (2000)

I absolutely want no part in any suggestions that our decision to use some electronic instruments is some kind of lifestyle choice. It's not. You use the instrument to help you get across a certain thing that you want to get across. That's all.
Thom (2000)

We're very lucky because of Jonny, my brother, he writes the strings and he can work with John Lubbock and the orchestra. We recorded them in this beautiful abbey which dates back to 1100 AD just near where our studio is in Oxford. So the ambience is beautiful and it's this group of musicians and they're not London session musicians. They're a private orchestra of people who don't like that world or that sort of playing… They were brilliant, and they were wonderful people.
Colin (2000)

There were some tenuous moments. There was this dissatisfaction with the way we used to work, but the new way – using computers more, using sequencers an awful lot – wasn't producing results.
Phil (2001)

We are delay and reverb snobs. I think the interesting thing is, we don't go for nice sounds… We can get up our own asses a bit, but what we do recognise is, when it comes to sounds, I think we've got quite good taste. We're good at judging what is and what is not a good sound. For us, part of recording is finding out different methodologies and techniques to create new sounds – which is what you should be doing in the recording studio.
Ed (2001)

'Dollars And Cents' is a live jam, but a live jam that's been cut up. And 'You And Whose Army' was basically a whole live performance.

But each song is different, like 'Packt Like Sardines' – straight out of Thom's laptop but we're playing it live with this distorted bass thing which is really exciting… a reverse archaeology is being practised upon the music, which is really cool.
Colin (2001)

Part of the thing about working with computers is you spend a lot of time seeing what works. And once you fall upon something you really like and feel is yours, you're quite loathe to give out all the information, because, well, you still have some use to be made of it, and you don't want someone nicking your idea. We want to surprise people and get the most out of the instruments, boxes, and stuff we're using. And the only way you do that is by not revealing anything.
Ed (2001)

The whole artifice of recording I see like this: a voice into a microphone onto a tape, onto your CD, through your speakers is all as illusory and fake as any synthesiser – it doesn't put Thom in your front room. But one is perceived as 'real', the other somehow 'unreal'… It's the same with guitars versus samplers. It was just freeing to discard the notion of acoustic sounds being truer.
Jonny (2001)

There are lots of different ways of making sound that don't require a guitar. Computer technology allows greater permutations in the sounds you can make.
Ed (2001)

spent years reading all these descriptions of them (Ondes Martenot, an exotic instrument), I couldn't even find a photograph, and then two years ago I finally got hold of one – and they're fantastic. The most famous use of the Martenot is the *Star Trek* theme, where it sounds like a woman singing. When it's played well, you can really emulate the voice. I get annoyed with electronic instruments because I reckon the Martenot is a bit of a peak.
Jonny (2001)

The Palm Speaker is something else that Monsieur Martenot invented, to go with the Ondes. It's a bit like a harp with a speaker in the middle of it. The strings are tuned to all 12 semitones of an octave, and when you play a note in tune, it resonates that specific string and it creates this weird kind of echo that's only on those pitches.
Jonny (2001)

People said *Kid A* was original, that it was radical or a departure or whatever, and I guess they meant it as a compliment – or they meant we'd gone off the rails, one of the two – but I was surprised. There just weren't as many guitars; it wasn't rocket science. It wasn't that amazingly original or different

at all. You're talking about developing certain techniques or using certain pieces of machinery or a new instrument, but once other people have learned to use it, okay, then you're no longer original. It usually doesn't take very long. Originality is completely subjective; one man's Pro Tools is another man's Marshall stack.
Thom (2001)

Computers butcher my work. They reproduce themselves without asking. They're never warm or friendly. The keys are in the wrong place. They don't go fast enough. They're heavy. They go out of date too fast. They're not loud enough. They're made by cheap labour. They keep changing the date to 1942 and then labelling all files accordingly. They never actually find the virus. They talk to each other but you can't hear. They are not logical.
Thom (2001)

I think guitars are over-idolised as instruments. All the guitarists I've ever liked have had the Bernard Sumner approach. It's about not practising. I like what Tom Waits said about only ever picking up an instrument if he's going to write a song.
Jonny (2001)

Boys Behaving Sensibly

I have a real problem being a man in the Nineties, anyway. Any man with any sensitivity or conscience toward the opposite sex would have a problem. To actually assert yourself in a masculine way without looking like you're in a hard-rock band is a very difficult thing to do... It comes back to the music we write, which is not effeminate, but it's not brutal in its arrogance. It's one of the things I'm always trying: to assert a sexual persona and, on the other hand, trying desperately to negate it.
Thom (1993)

I've never taken advantage of the opportunity of one-night stands. It's like treating sex like sneezing. Sex is a fairly disgusting sort of tufted, smelly-area kind of activity, which is too intimate to engage in with strangers. I'm all for erotic in terms of imagination, but the physical side is something different.
Jonny (1995)

I'm sure we'd probably all be much happier and better party monsters if we indulged in Class A drugs, but we'd probably self-destruct six months down the line, which is what a lot of bands do. I'm not defending or condoning bands' use of drugs, it is a bizarre, precarious, insecure, paranoid, falsely-comfortable, perspective-distorting lifestyle. Personally, we've never been a band to focus any energies in groupies or drugs or anything like that. I mean, I

don't know any bands that do, to be honest – maybe I don't see it. We're quite a solitary band, but everyone is so different; you talk to each member of the band and you get a different answer.
Colin (1995)

We're not purposefully contradictory. It just happens that we like to use our brains. If you consider what you're doing at all important, you'll pay more attention to it and not just get drunk 'round the pub until it's time to get on stage.
Thom (1995)

We were all brought up in middle-class Oxford, and there's an air of politeness that's hard to escape.
Ed (1995)

We could have tried to do this when we were 18 or 19, but finishing school was important to us. It was a good decision because at university you learn how to think for yourself.
Ed (1995)

I think part of it is not living in London, having success elsewhere, the kind of people we are; we stick together and don't really listen to anyone else. We're just quietly learning what we do and getting better. It's all an ongoing process, I think it takes a long time to understand the medium in which you work. We didn't just wake up one morning and decide to be Mods.
Thom (1995)

I think the most unhealthy thing for a human being is to feel that they have to behave in a certain way because other people expect them to, or to feel they have to think in a certain way.
Thom (1995)

It barely pays the bills, really, but what's really scary is when you start hearing people saying things like, 'At least you don't have to work for a living', and it's 'Fuck, yeah!' You forget that… We are fucking lucky.
Thom (1995)

I feel I'm in an immense position of privilege to be able to stand back and watch things happen. The most unhealthy thing to think is you have to prove your work outside of what you do. You don't. My girlfriend has this quote in her sketchbook: 'Remain orderly in your life so you can be free and chaotic in your work.' I think basically you lose it when you destroy your brain or destroy yourself emotionally or burn yourself up.
Thom (1996)

It's much better to come from that angle, where people think you're readers of books and bridge players, because it means they don't have rock'n'roll expectations. We camped that up to an enormous extent in '93 or whenever, purposely. And we don't get hassle from customs.
Ed (1998)

They do these little cans of Guinness over here. They're quite sweet. I'll have one of those after the show. I'm getting less rock'n'roll as the tour goes on.
Colin (1998)

When you're back at home, there are an awful lot of domestic matters to deal with, and when you're on tour you're removed from those. But if there's someone at home actually dealing with them for you, it sends you on a guilt trip. We're all aware of what a mess we leave behind us.
Phil (1998)

We all had to start from the beginning again for the new album which was really hard and it took a long time. Also we spent a lot of time rebuilding our private lives as well after being away a lot, because we didn't want to end up like sad casualties of rock in our thirties... sort of with a nice income but with no friends or family. We concentrated on that. We went home, and that was important.
Colin (2000)

Our lifestyles are not really extravagant. We don't live in really big houses and we don't have all that stuff to support. If there is any point in carrying on we have to do things in such a way that we find interesting and different and creative and stimulating and short.
Colin (2000)

Hopefully, this'll be the last time rock musicians are allowed to behave like idiots and get away with it. For me, that's dull. They should all go home, and get a life and go and listen to something else. I don't think that's sour grapes because I'm over 30.
Thom (2000)

I think one of the good things, one of the cool things about being in a band is it gives the opportunity to talk about what you're into on a wider scale than just down the pub with your friends. But you have to be careful that it doesn't become an egotistical rant. That'll really turn people off.
Colin (2001)

Insults And Injury

People sometimes ask me if I'm happy and I tell them to fuck off. If I was happy, I'd be in a fucking car advert. A lot of people think they're happy, and then they live these boring lives and do the same things every day. But one day they wake up and realise they haven't lived yet. I'd much rather celebrate the highs and lows of everyday life than try to deny them.
Thom (1995)

Our so-called success in America allowed us to do lots of things, but it also meant that somehow we owed somebody something. But I couldn't work out who and I couldn't work out how much.
Thom (1997)

When the show came round, people had driven hundreds of miles to come and it was snowing and it was like three or four foot deep and I just thought: 'There is no way I'm not doing the show because these people have travelled this far'. So I got up on stage and I thought it would be all right, but after three songs I lost my voice completely and I was croaking and got really fucking freaked out. I got tunnel vision and I don't really know what happened. I threw stuff around and threw my amp around and drum kit and ended up with blood all over my face and things. I cried for about two hours afterwards.
I want people to know what

happened that night. I'm sure no one gives a fuck and I'm sure the *New Musical Express* don't give a fuck, but what they wrote in that piece hurt me more than anything else anyone has ever written about me.
Thom (1995)

My ear was ringing and bleeding for two weeks on an American tour. There was this terrifying gig in Cleveland, where I was nearly fainting. I was taken to hospital at three in the morning and the doctor said the situation was really grim.
Ed (1997)

On the day (of recording *Kid A*'s 'The National Anthem') I said to them, 'You know when you've been in a traffic jam for four hours and if someone says the wrong thing to you, you'll just kill 'em, you'll fucking snap and probably throttle them?... Any tiny spark and you're going to go off, and you're in the midst of two or three hundred other people who are in exactly the same thing. I wanted them to play like that, like, this fucking close to going off lynching or killing, it's like a mob just about to spark off.
Jonny and I were conducting it, and we ran through it a few times and people started to get ideas, and it was such a great day! I broke my foot, actually, because I was jumping up and down so much.
Thom (2000)

On the last tour, my back was out for most of the time and I could hardly bend down; I had to take painkillers a lot… The reasons were complicated, but had to do with the flailing around I was doing.
Thom (2001)

Songwriting And Recording

We joined this band to write songs and be musicians, but we spent a year being a jukebox instead. We felt, creatively, in a kind of stasis for a year and a half because we couldn't release anything new.
Jonny (1995)

If I'm happy I don't usually write. I'm happy after I write. There's an enormous sense of release. But I don't feel that we have to carry on churning out songs that are all about desperate human beings at the end of their tether, la-la-la. That's all a bit old and boring now. It's a fine line between writing something with genuine emotional impact and turning into little idiots feeling sorry for ourselves and playing stadium rock.
Thom (1995)

We were playing like paranoid little mice in cages, not us playing like we play normally. We were so frightened, so shit-scared about getting this record right. Every act and every note you played was a real major deal.
Thom (1995)

You can actually record anywhere, but it's mixing that is the important thing. You should mix quietly – people who mix their tracks at ear-splitting volume really don't have a clue. We go through an hour mixing quietly, take a break, then come back to it and listen to it really

fucking loud, then turn it back down again.
Thom (1993)

It can be an exiting and fast way of working. Just throw a load of your drumming on tape and slice it up. I suppose some people would think that I was bit of a cheat – but what's a cheat if you can respond emotionally and it's good music?
Phil (1996)

For me, the problem with recording came when I suddenly became conscious of all the things that could go wrong. I stopped listening to my musical voice and I froze up. The studio can be a nightmarish situation for any drummer. The session can't go ahead until you've got your drum part down.
Phil (1996)

A lot of it is down to publicity. A lot of it is down to luck. You've got absolutely no idea that anybody's going to get it. I'm convinced that all the songs we've written at the moment, all the new songs, that nobody is going to get it. Maybe little bits, glimpses – they might get that. But basically, they're not going to get it.
Thom (1996)

This whole thing, the science of the studio, is very much an Eighties phenomenon, where everything had to be close-miked. But that's

not how you hear a drum kit as a complete instrument itself. In the Eighties they tried to conjure up some mystique about working in the studio; but the mystique is not about what you do in the studio. It's in your performance.
Phil (1996)

Recording studios now tend to be quite scientific and clinical. You can't really impose yourself without getting over the fact that there are fag burns in the carpet and gold discs all around.
Jonny (1997)

If you don't have any semblance of a normal life, then you won't be able to write – and if you can't write, then you won't be there.
Thom (1997)

For the whole of the year when we were recording *OK Computer*, we were incredibly privileged . The record company visited us twice, and they were short visits. Just being given that trust – it's your ideal position. And I think people are very envious of our position at the moment. *OK Computer* is only our third album – that kind of treatment is usually reserved for bands with much more experience.
Phil (1998)

What we'd do is half-finish 14 songs, and then go on to a new one. We get bored very, very quickly. So, by Christmas, it was basically that we wanted an album out by the summer, and we had to finish it off.
Ed (1998)

The problem is that we are essentially in limbo. For the first time… we have nothing to get ready for, except 'an album', but we've been working on that since January and nothing substantial has come of it, except maybe a few harsh lessons in how not to do things… Are we going down Stone Roses territory?
Ed – web diary entry during recording of Kid A (1999)

One of the ambitions of this album is working with other musicians. Like we've got these great horn players we worked with as well on 'The National Anthem'. And establishing a relationship with these people so we can work with them again rather than what normally happens if you're a band and you do a string session. You finish the album and then you take the song and you want the strings and you take it to Abbey Road or wherever and you stick it on and they just play on top of it.
We want to try and incorporate the strings into the music earlier and ultimately what we'd like to do is we want Thom to sing or get members of the band to play at the same time as the strings are being recorded like Scott Walker in the Sixties… The ambience of a room with everyone playing together. That's one of our ambitions.
Colin (2000)

A lot of the songwriting now isn't really about songwriting at all, it's about editing, building up a lot of material, then piecing it together

like a painter. But it's weird approaching that with vocals, because all the stuff I've been listening to, almost none of it has vocals. That was one of the things that I was most interested in; that I was so in love with this music, yet there wasn't much vocal interpretation.
Thom (2000)

If you're going to make a different-sounding record, you have to change the methodology. And it's scary – everyone feels insecure. I'm a guitarist and suddenly it's like, 'Well, there are no guitars on this track, or no drums'. Jonny, me, Coz and Phil had to get our heads round that. Would we survive with our egos intact?
Ed (2000)

The track ('The National Anthem') evolved over two years, and when you record a track over that amount of time, you forget what's good about it. The drums and bass were done at the end of '97 when we finished the UK tour for *OK Computer*, and we went into the studio to do some B-sides. We didn't pick up the track again until last summer in Gloucestershire, and then we had a brass section come in sometime in November '99. It's a very ill-disciplined way of recording. But it's actually a very interesting way of working, because you're adding things to the stew – as well as rejecting things – and then you come back to the song with fresh ears.
Ed (2001)

I honestly didn't feel I had a role to play. My suggestion for *OK Computer*'s follow-up had been to say, 'Let's go back to the well-crafted three-and-a-half minute song'. I came from idolising The Smiths in the Eighties and I thought that would be the shocking thing to do. It was really difficult because, as a musician, I express myself more emotionally than cerebrally. The other problem was the lyrics. Whenever we'd done a record before, Thom's lyrics were evolving. He'd give you sheets and once you see the words to, say, 'No Surprises', you immediately think, 'Ah yes, we need a guitar for this that sounds like a child's musical box'. This time, there were no lyrics and therefore no reference points. Phil, Colin and I went through some major dilemmas at various stages. How could we contribute to this new music? We all wondered if it wasn't better to just walk away. It was a very scary thing at first.
Ed (2001)

It did my head in that whatever I did with my voice, it had that particular set of associations. And there were lots of similar bands coming out at the time, and that made it even worse. I couldn't stand the sound of me. I got really into the idea of my voice being another one of the instruments, rather than this precious, focus thing all the time.
Thom (2001)

The more concerts we do, the more dissatisfied we get with trying to reproduce the live sound on a record. In a way it can't be done, and that's a relief really, when you accept that, and recording just becomes a different thing.
Jonny (2001)

It really did take us too long to get these recordings done. We've had our rough times in the studio in the past, but after four weeks most of the material would have been recorded. This time it seemed like it just goes on and on. Another problem was that most of the time in the studio we weren't playing together, as a band. After a few months like this you miss it, just standing and playing together.
Ed (2001)

He (producer Nigel Godrich) is just great and he's a lovely man and, you know, he's a friend so you just want the best for your friends. And he has an overall sense of fair play which he brings to Radiohead as well, which is a really important quality when you're dealing with a group of five people who have their own power-based relationships and political relationships built up over working together for 15 years.
Colin (2001)

Nigel is very into this idea that if you're going to do something weird with a track, you make it weird there and then, rather than doing it in the mix afterwards, because the effect changes the way people play. They'll play to it. And that's really inspiring, because it's like having a new instrument. If you've got an incredibly cool reverb or

something on your voice, suddenly you're really excited about what you're doing again.
Jonny (2001)

I think the whole definition of what it means to be a producer is becoming increasingly curious and questionable in terms of how bands record and whether bands exist and technology's so cheap now and you can record things on your computer and all of that kind of stuff. It just comes down to the personal relationships you have with the person who's recording your music. That's what it comes down, really. And getting on with people. It's like being in a band.
We definitely don't have any plans to stop working with him (Nigel), if he wants to still work with us. It's really exciting 'cause it's nice to have re-mixes done by other people. So that whole area is open to us as well as a continued relationship with the excellent Nigel Godrich.
Colin (2001)

Thom with Brian Eno
at the Brit Awards, 1996.

The Biz

I was always interested in the way bands were set up, as much as in the music. We wanted to stay in control like, say, REM. For us, that's paramount. We're not rock'n'roll idiots or sad cases.
Ed (1993)

The big British labels are all owned by conglomerates now. Rupert Perry of EMI is answerable to the Thorn EMI board. Bands build up large debts touring – we did, but you build up a fanbase – but after the second record, the company could say, 'You're too expensive, we're getting rid of you'. There are no visionaries in the British business any more.
Ed (1994)

What frightens me is the idea that what Radiohead do is basically packaged back to people in the form of entertainment, to play in their car stereos on their way to work. And that's not why I started this but then I should shut the fuck up because it's pop music and it's not anything more than that. But I got into music because I naively thought that pop music was basically the only viable art-form left, because the art world is run by a few very extremely privileged people and is ultimately corrupt and barren of any context. And I thought that the pop music industry was different… I was fucking wrong.
Thom (1995)

What worries me most is that having toured places like Mexico and Thailand, MTV is like this cultural symbol that introduces you and I don't think I can handle being a part of that. They're flying around dropping little cultural bombs saying 'Here you are, eat this'.
Thom (1995)

I just get really wound up because I think that when we got involved in what we do, we were so naive. I still think we are naive and I used to sort of want to hide it and now I'm proud of it because I think the most offensive thing about the music business, the most offensive thing about the media in general, is the level of cynicism and the fact that people really believe that they can pawn off endlessly recycled bullshit with no heart and people will buy it. And people do buy it, so I'm wrong and they're right.
Thom (1995)

I went to the Brit Awards and I saw… a lot of women who couldn't fit in their cocktail dresses and lots of men in black ties who essentially didn't want to be there, but were. And I was there and we were all committing the same offence. All my favourite artists are people who never seem to be involved in the industry. I found myself getting involved in it, and I felt really ashamed to be there.
Thom (1995)

We spent most of the night (Brit Awards) talking to Massive Attack and Tricky because they were at the tables nearby, and we got on with them really well. But there was a lot of booing that night that got edited out on the television. It made me feel pretty ashamed to be part of it.
Thom (1996)

You do sometimes get the feeling that you're just one more element in the entertainment industry's desperate attempt to distract people from the fact that their lives are messed up.
Thom (1996)

I got into the music business thinking it was really radical, that it wasn't really a business at all, that it was a lot of people being artistic and creative. Not true, and it made me very depressed.
Thom (1996)

Every time you do a record, you're blackmailed into going on tour for two years, which is bollocks. It's all part of the promotional, marketing campaign, you see.
Thom (1998)

When I say you've got an audience in mind, you don't look at sales figures but you do play it to your friends in Oxford, and if they think you've completely lost it, then they're probably right. **Jonny (1998)**

I get very suspicious when bands say they don't think about their audience and they do music for themselves. I never really believe that, I mean, it always feels to me like we are doing music for the people who bought our last record and if they don't understand what we are doing now, or if they hate what we are doing now then we've gone wrong, I think.
Jonny (1998)

It's funny: you're sort of permanently in debt in a way, because the record company fund your record, and you pay them back with the sales, and the following year they give you another lump of money that's got to fund you for the next year, and has got to pay for the recording and all the touring. It's good, you feel like you're in gainful employment and things carry on.
Jonny (1998)

The thing that really did my head in was going home and turning on the TV and the ads for fucking banks and cars being more like MTV videos than the MTV videos: it seemed like there was nowhere to go. Whatever the new aesthetic was would be in a fucking car advert a week later. Especially Colin, he got obsessed over not making videos and making adverts. Because the ads were more like the videos, so we might as well go straight to the source. You're lying if you're pretending that it's not a product, that you're not trying to sell something. It wasn't like we sat down and said, 'How do we do things differently?' Necessity meant that we had to.
Thom (2000)
They're just cheap TV ads, they always were cheap TV ads. I mean, in the context of MTV, although we owe them a lot, the whole MTV thing and what it did to music, it just got way out of hand…
It was a nightmare, and it took years, literally, because you feel like you've got nowhere to go and every day you think, 'Well, maybe we should just stop? Maybe there's no point to this', because all the sounds you made, that made you happy, have been sucked of everything they meant. It's a total headfuck. And you've got no one to blame.
Thom (2000)

I always wanted whatever I did to end up in the high street, no matter what it was, because to me, there isn't anywhere else to go. It's pointless.
Thom (2000)

Rock music sucks, I hate it! I'm so fucking bored of it, I hate it! It's a fucking waste of time. It's not really the music, it's not sitting on a stage playing guitar, drums and singing, that's not what I'm talking about. What I'm talking about is all the mythology that goes with it. I've got a real fucking problem with that! I've got a real problem with the idea you have to tour yourself stupid, do certain things, talk to certain people. I totally snapped.
I think it's the same as with literature and art. A lot of time you confuse the personality with the piece of work. Ultimately it doesn't do anybody any favours. It negates the work as well. What can happen essentially if you're an artist like Rothko and you chose to kill yourself, that colours the work forever more, which is totally not the point and it destroys the work. There's a Rothko room in the Tate Gallery in London, when kids go in there they go, 'Wow, this is great!' and all they see is the colour and the joy of the paintings. And all the adults see is this poor sod that killed himself.
Thom (2000)

In '97, I went around slagging every single awards ceremony off, and at that time, I felt like, you know, I didn't, we didn't want to go to them. But you know, we're human beings, we change what we feel about them… You know, we've been offered like the chance to come over to LA for five days, put up in a great hotel, go to parties, and it's kinda like, you know, you know, we want to see it, we want to do this once, we want to see what it's like going to a few parties… we might not enjoy it… we may well not, but, you know, you gotta try these things.
Ed (2001)

We never had some master plan. It was more like 'what do we want to do this time?' We didn't want to do singles or videos. If you look at the singles market in the UK at the moment it's just pop. It's good, but it's just not where we would want to be.
Ed (2001)

It was a weird feeling, because you are right at the sharp end of the sexy, sassy, MTV eye-candy lifestyle thing that they're trying to sell to the rest of the world, make them aspire to. It's fair enough to question it. Unfortunately, if you're interested in actually being heard, you have to work within the system.
Thom (2001)

The Road

First and foremost, Radiohead is a live band. The best way to get into Radiohead is to see them live. It's very passionate, it's very intense. It's not the type of gig where you sit in the back and drink and have a chat. You will see five guys totally absorbed on stage in what they're playing.
Ed (1993)

It's a weird situation to be in. To be the stadium rock band it's okay to like. The whole Phil Spector thing, huge-sounding instruments. For me it's so much more evocative. It's not because we want to change the world. It's simply because the other side to that is it's a reaction against everything else we're hearing.
Thom (1995)

We were quite ready to climb the walls. We were trapped in the studio, recording and re-recording. It didn't seem like the songs could really grow on us until we started playing them live for people.
Phil (1995)

We've always been in it for the long haul, if you like, and to be associated with any kind of a scene is something we've been keen to avoid. When people come to a Radiohead gig, it's a little bit of a secret, it's still word of mouth. I think when people come to hear us live, it's like, 'I must tell someone' – and that's the way we've always wanted to do it.
Ed (1995)

R.E.M.

We did some shows with Beck about two or three weeks ago and the only song I'd heard, obviously, was 'Loser'; his 'Loser' was like our 'Creep'. I didn't buy the album and I saw him live and he was brilliant. It's when you go see a band live, that's when you can tell if they're going to cut it or not.
Ed (1995)

We did this large tour with James in Europe. A lot of it was like, 'Yeah, we're the support band' and you could go on stage and make a complete prick of yourself and the more the better, which I enjoyed doing for several months.
The first show we did (after that) was in a really dirty club. There were three tiny wooden tables that were used as a barricade. The only way off stage in the back was through a little window, and it was about as different an experience (from the James tour) as humanly possible.
Thom (1995)

The only time I feel comfortable is when I'm in front of a mike. I'm obsessed with the idea that I'm completely losing touch with who I am, and I've come to the conclusion that there isn't anything to Thom Yorke other than the guy that makes those painful songs.
Thom (1995)

We needed to play live. We stopped recording our new record, *The Bends*, and toured Southeast Asia for two months. We found crowds there latched on quickly to our new material.
Ed (1995)

Watching R.E.M. was very interesting because they've always been one of those bands who haven't been scared to rehearse the song maybe once and then do it in front of 25,000 people. I think that's really cool and I want us to be able to do that. We go 'Oh no, I need to rehearse it another two or three times'.
It would be great if we got to that stage, and think, 'Fuck it, if we fuck up in front of 25,000 people it's not going to make that much difference because people aren't going to hold that against you'. For me, watching R.E.M. proves that, because they're human, that's brilliant, that's so cool.
Ed (1995)

It was bizarre. We were discussing whether we could get away with sounding like R.E.M. the rest of our lives, and now they've asked us to open for them.
Jonny (1995)

The only other person I've ever talked to about this is Michael Stipe and he just said, 'It takes me six months to come down from a tour at least, now, or more than that', so I can understand it. All the emotions and all the tensions and the freak-outs are all stocked up and they all come seeping out at the end so you have to keep it together. It's the same with the live situation. Sometimes I think it's just amusing and it's just a joke and I just enjoy that rather than fighting it any longer.
Thom (1995)

This year we're mixing touring with recording. For us, that's a really good blend. Each side seeps into the other, and you can always keep a good check on your progress as you go along.
Phil (1996)

I can't see why we're doing these big gigs. Thing is, whoever it is up there, it's not the person sitting here. It's a completely different state of mind that you have to spend a long time getting into. I can't switch it on and off. When even the logistics of these big gigs are discussed, I just fucking freeze up. It's not something I'm emotionally capable of dealing with yet. Hopefully I'll get back into a different frame of mind where it won't worry me.
Thom (1997)

Have I ever fallen flat on my arse? Oh yeah, definitely. But as long as the hit rate is over 70 per cent, I'll carry on playing like that.
Jonny (1998)

The best thing about this is the way that people come up to us now and say, 'I was at Glastonbury'. There was a friend of mine who's seen us a million times, ever since we started, and he was up in the hills, stoned out of his face with all these old people in tents that he didn't really know, and he said everyone was turning around saying, 'This is where we're all at, right now.' Apocalypse Now. It was Apocalypse Now. We were running on pure blind terror when we went on.
Thom (1998)

No one wants to play solos or takes a lead, really.
Jonny (1998)

I thrive on the movement on tour. The travelling around is a big part of it for me. There's lots going on every day, and if you go home you tend to obsess more.
Thom (1998)

I don't think there's anything worthy in going on tour for two years. You just turn yourself into a fucking maniac. And then you have to turn yourself back.
Thom (1998)

Now we want to play music in interesting places and in towns or countries we have never visited before. When we receive new reactions to our music, we become excited and we get a lot of inspiration and that's what makes us create new stuff.
Phil (2000)

When you go on tour, it's a little like a military exercise! It is necessary to think several months of it in advance. More especially we wanted to play in interesting places. That's why we chose the antic theatres in the South and Le Grand Rex in Paris. We made our decision last February, and we had not even finished the album (*Kid A*). We still had ten weeks of work remaining. It was like a way of giving us a cut-off date for the recording. More especially as we did not have any limit of time imposed for this disc and we had started work a year ago.
Ed (2000)

I would especially like to be able to take time to appreciate all that is fantastic to be found in a foreign country. What had disappointed me at the time of the last tour, was to go on a worldwide tour, we were in some incredible places and we couldn't enjoy it, hadn't the time.

In June and July, we arranged ourselves to be able to have a more human pace. And then, we will play beautiful places, in the open air or in theatres.
Ed (2000)

When you're playing to 8,000 people, there are going to be people who just want you to play out-and-out rock, but people hopefully know us better now, know that we won't do that. We might do a little bit; we played 'The Bends' tonight, which we haven't played for two years…
Ed (2000)

If you ask any band, the difference between starting a tour in Britain or Europe is immense. You know that when you open up in the UK, there are always people who come along in a sceptical frame of mind, whereas in Europe it's more like, 'Thanks for coming'. It's a good and bad thing but, as Brits, we're very, very critical and we have this love of people fucking up. We do, it's true…
Ed (2000)

When we were touring around *Pablo Honey* and 'Creep' we expected to get back in the studio (in) six months and it was like two-and-a-half years later. It's like being stuck in a room with one picture that you have to look at for two-and-a-half years and you can't do anything, you haven't got any materials to do anything else. You know, you want to try and be a moving target, and concentrate on quality, really.
Colin (2001)

This time around we're playing these concerts in the summer in beautiful places in France and Italy and Greece and Israel. And then we're coming back and playing concerts in September. It's more relaxed. It's just we got to the stage in our lives where we decided we had to enjoy it otherwise there wasn't any point in doing it because we weren't interested in just doing it for the money.
Colin (2000)

A lot of *Meeting People Is Easy* (the documentary film of Radiohead's world tour) is set in Japan and what you don't see is, after we finish in Japan it was after two weeks of touring and it was winter and snow and we were very tired. Japan is a wonderful country but if you're there for longer than a week or so, it's a very oppressive culture, in terms of the language, you can't understand anything. It messes with your head in a weird way. I love it but after a while you feel like an innocent alien.

Then we went to New Zealand and Australia and, of course, it was summer. We were like swimming in the sea, and barbecues and drinking, going go-kart racing... If Grant (the director) had come and shot that, then everyone would have seen us being like the Monkees.

Colin (2000)

(*Meeting People Is Easy*) does articulate what we're trying to say about being stuck on this sort of treadmill. And it's offensive. Because if you're in Japan and you're doing these things and you're not enjoying it, then you shouldn't be doing it because it's such a privilege to be there. No one wants to be like that. Like hating where you are... that's terrible. Because one of the great gifts about this job is being able to travel and if you can't enjoy that then you shouldn't go.

Colin (2000)

Grant is a good director, but he only showed the negative side of the tour (on *Meeting People Is Easy*). He recorded a lot in Japan, where we'd only been for two weeks. It was cold, it snowed, we couldn't read or understand the culture. We were going crazy. After Japan we went to Australia and New Zealand where it was sunny and warm.

We went swimming and go-kart racing, we were invited to barbecues and had big fun. Grant wasn't there. The film only shows 25 per cent of what was really going on. If it was always as bad as in the film, we wouldn't be in this band. That's why we want to do this Tent tour. Because we never want to be in a situation in which we feel sorry for ourselves!
Colin (2000)

A lot of the songs we'd never played live before. It was the first time we had songs on a record that had been completely constructed in the studio and had not been endlessly toured and rehearsed. We had to change the form of some of them to make sure they worked live, and on the whole I think they did.
Ed (2000)

Flexibility is what we need, a piece of land and permission from the authorities to put a tent on it. You don't have to plan things a year ahead. This way we have more freedom. It's a lazy tour in beautiful surroundings with two days off in between the gigs. We've reached the point that the quality of our performances and the fun we have is most important.
We could have been the headliner on most of the European festivals and earn a lot of money. But then this tour would have been just as annoying as the tour after *OK Computer*, and I don't think the band would survive that. Thom couldn't put himself through that again. And neither could I.
Colin (2000)

Our problem is we want to control everything… it's almost depressing! At all events, even if the capacity is 10,000 people, it will be an intimate place, which was really significant for us. There will also be lights adapted to the place.
Ed (2000)

We didn't run at a profit on that tour (the Tent tour). We just wanted to provide something different; a better experience than you'd have got in your Wembley Arenas or wherever. That cost us money.
Ed (2000)

I had real horrors about the tent and everything, I thought we were crazy.
Thom (2000)

People concentrated on the lack of banners and advertising and that was just a by-product of having your own venue. We were never going to get obsessed by whether the beer tent had logos in it. The concept was what was worrying us.
Jonny (2000)

Having the same tent every night meant we didn't have to compromise – the sound and lights were amazing, they're the best gigs we have ever done. But I do accept tickets were dear. We may go back to Brixton-style venues and only charge half-price. Some people always assume that we know 'the right thing to do' – the truth is, we don't.
Ed (2001)

There has to be some kind of focus. Where that is for us is when we play live, really, and I think when people come and see our concerts, that helps a lot to see how everything fits together and make sense of it. It's really important for us and I don't think we'd really work as a band if we didn't have that live performance. That interaction with the audience is the ultimate form of accountability and that's good. One of the reasons we did the music on these two records in this way was to try and make things a bit more fluid and less verse-chorus-verse and so to try and keep a level of interest for us when we play it so that it's always more authentic and less repetitive when we perform in front of an audience.
Colin (2001)

We'd observed with horror that every band's second or third album would always have a song called 'Motel Ain't Home' or 'No Place Like Home', and bands usually succumb to that, but we're still enjoying it.
Ed (1995)

A lot of bands can't stand tour buses, but we're the opposite. It's that gang thing, isn't it? It's like you're going camping for two weeks. But it's on a bus. It's a bit sad really.
Thom (1995)

We spent so long on the road after 'Creep' that we felt like we were digging ourselves into a rut. We worried we may not have anything left to say, but eventually we came up with the new songs. We're stronger as a unit now than we've ever been.
Ed (1995)

It's like being one of those Russian astronauts who stayed out circling the Earth for a year in a metal fuselage – it's a physical and emotional challenge. The only constructive element is the limbo aspect – it's quite useful for writing and reading and general brain stuff.
(1995)

Stars And Stripes

When you're promoting your record there (the US), you have to do things you don't do here, like meet the people who distribute your record to shops. Many English bands think they're above all that, and they're all po-faced when they do it. We went over with curiosity about the place, and combined it with a work ethic.
Ed (1994)

It's a great song. We love it and still play it. But we became known in America as the 'Creep' band instead of Radiohead.
Ed (1995)

Americans have this thing about confessing. You can meet someone in a bar and within a few minutes you find out they've had three abortions and split up with two husbands. You've been talking to a complete stranger and you know all this stuff. There's this bizarre confessional aspect which I'm kind of into sometimes when I write, and I think that's what they pick up on.
Thom (1995)

It's amusing to watch new British acts shoved at Americans, but at the same time it's sad, because it's to the detriment of true musicians. We have this running joke that we've successfully managed to miss every scene by at least half a year. So now we don't even bother.
Thom (1995)

There's this assumption that Radiohead are big in America. Radiohead are not big in America. We had 'Fake Plastic Trees' as a single and it was played to a radio station. They did a survey of their listeners – 18-to-25-year-old males who drive four-wheel-drive jeeps – and it came bottom of the list. The thing with Radiohead and America is that we had one pop hit there.
Ed (1997)

At that time the whole so-called alternative rock thing had happened there (in the US), populated by sap programmers from the Eighties who didn't have a clue what they were putting on and 'Creep' suffered from that. It was a good song, but afterwards it was, well, let's have more of that please because the programmers understand it, and it's like, 'no, sorry'.
Thom (1997)

There were so many elements to that period. It was such a weird trip anyway, because suddenly we were seen as this big investment and there was money being thrown at us. It didn't last long enough to mess us up, but then I suppose, for a while, it probably did.
Thom (1997)

We didn't know what was normal in America. We went over there and we'd turn on MTV and 'Creep' would be on again. We though, 'Oh, that's good'.
Jonny (1997)

People were being very nice to us over there because 'Creep' was doing well. 'Stop Whispering' didn't do quite so well, so that opened us up to the more cynical side of it.
Phil (1997)

Well it's funny, because they (their US record company) made a prediction of how many records they planned to sell of *OK Computer* before they heard the record. And then they heard the record, and cut the prediction in a half or a quarter, I think. So that's never been a problem with us. They've never overly hyped us, or expected much from us.
Jonny (1998)

Obviously when you get great theatres, it would be lovely to do a residency for three nights, but America is such a huge country that you wouldn't have the luxury of that. If you've got one night, you don't want people to not get in.
Ed (1998)

I tell you what's funny, with 'Optimistic' we've had our biggest radio hit over there since 'Creep'. Music sounds different in America, especially on the radio because of the compression. Something happens to 'Optimistic' when you put it through the radio compression on those FM stations over there and suddenly it sounds like an American rock song.
Ed (2000)

It really was great. We had two weeks over there and we were feted and taken places and did *Saturday Night Live*. Americans love success, so if you've got a Number 1 record they really, really like you. The shows in New York and LA were just surreal.
Ed (2000)

We only spent two weeks there (the USA), but we really liked it. The press was really nice, which made a change. There's much less questioning in America. The highlight of the whole *Kid A* thing was our *Saturday Night Live* performance. I was so proud of that. I was walking on water for a week after that – I felt so good. That was a real achievement. *SNL* is notoriously intimidating. We heard all these terrible horror stories from Michael (Stipe) about it.
Thom (2001)

Life And Death

By this time I'm supposed to have fucked myself up permanently, or be dead. I'm supposed to be so fucked up now that I can't work any more. You can get precious about things. I just try to go with however I feel at the moment, otherwise I start writing agendas.

Once we finished this record (*Kid A*) I started being easier on myself, because I understood a little bit better where I was supposed to be. All the way through I was faced with the prospect of thinking, 'Maybe it'll never happen.' I managed to get sounds that I wanted out of my head and onto tape as much as we could, and that meant I could be a little bit happier about the place I was at.
Thom (2000)

It's a fear of dying, actually. It's a 30-thing. Most men hit 30 and think, 'Oh my God, I'm not immortal'. Definitely fear of dying on *Kid A*. A lot of that going on.
Thom (2000)

I have this house down by the sea and the landscape around it is really harsh, brutal. I used to just go off for the whole day, walking, and just feeling totally like nothing. Thinking I'll be back in the ground as soon as I know it. It's all just corny stuff, and when you sit down and talk about it, it all sounds like complete bollocks.
Thom (2000)

Coldplay's Chris Martin

The idea of dying unprepared… is very frightening. Not having time to say goodbye. It seems just insane. Cars have lost the romance we grew up swallowing. Now they are just personal protection spaces, somewhere to sit in traffic and wait or play with death against complete strangers. I used to be really, really bad about saying goodbye to people when they got in their cars. I still insist that my friends ring me when they get home to tell me they're safe. But I used to be much worse. I would be frantic if someone was unusually late. The absolute worst thing about touring is insane taxi drivers with no seat belts in busy cities. I also find it very difficult to accept lifts from somebody. Just like Mummy told me.
Thom (2001)

A heart is obviously completely useless unless you are in a country and western song. A brain can stay alive even when you're clinically dead and can be used to useful ends such as operating train signals and reading books. If the power fails, it can be hooked up to a car battery or a transformer. A brain pulsates in dramatic fashion when preserved in a bubbling glass container, and there have been cases of a brain holding complete power over an entire nation.
Thom (2001)

Jarvis Cocker

Other Opinions

We know this is a band with a future, not a one-hit wonder.
Tom Curson, Capitol Records artist development (1993)

Radiohead are so good, they scare me.
R.E.M.'s Michael Stipe (1995)

I often cried with Radiohead. I remember one time, during the recording of 'Fake Plastic Trees', Thom Yorke was singing with nothing else than his acoustic guitar – it was deeply moving. When he sings, he's as intense in an empty studio as he could be in front of a 20,000 people crowd. Then again, in everyday life, he's a very funny and adorable guy.
Producer Nigel Godrich (2000)

It's Radiohead: a band that will never get out of fashion, because they make the fashion. And when the others follow, they are already somewhere else, far away.
Nigel Godrich (2000)

Thom was doing his vocals and he'd have vanished from view altogether. He'd be sitting cross-legged in some sort of meditative posture at the bottom of the vocal booth.
Jazz trumpeter Humphrey Lyttleton, who worked with the band on 'Amnesiac' (2001).

I've liked some of their stuff – really adventurous.
Paul Weller (2001)

I love 'em. Had the pleasure of playing with them a few years ago and they were lovely.
Alanis Morissette (2001)

I really like them. They've made an effort to be different. If they did the same thing over again people would complain.
Pulp's Jarvis Cocker (2001)

They're amazing.
Coldplay's Chris Martin (2001)

They're great. They've saved their career by not making the same record over and over again.
R.E.M.'s Peter Buck (2001)

They're truly special. They're going to be making exciting music for a long time.
U2's Adam Clayton (2001)

Beck

The Future

The questions will always be asked, 'Are we still enjoying it? Are we actually doing something different? Are we gaining from doing this?' If we're going over old ground, there's no point doing it. We're obviously not doing it to maintain some kind of lifestyle, because we don't have those kind of lifestyles. You've got to keep learning. And the other thing is, you've got to enjoy it. It was like, 'Fucking hell – you get to 32 years old, and if you're not enjoying it…'
Ed (2000)

The trick is to try and carry on doing things that interest you, but not turn into some awful art-rock nonsense for its own sake so that it looks like you're cutting your nose off to spite your face. For me, what I hope we end up being is like a West Coast group that does a record every year, or somebody like The Beta Band where the work is of very high quality and you have a bedrock of support and respect.
Colin (2000)

We're embarking on a new route. We couldn't have carried on like the way it was before. There was absolutely no point. It's a cliché, but what we've done is split the band up and reform it with the same five members: You know, I think one of the most important ethics of Radiohead is that we're not nostalgic. We never talk about school. We were all at school together, but we never look back. We never talk about what we've done in the past.
Ed (2000)

Basically bands get screwed by record companies. That's a fact. And that's all going to change: with the onset of on-line distribution, the whole way that music is made will change. 78s dictated the way music was made, then 45s, then 33s, then CDs – it's all changed. Now, wouldn't it be great to do a track a month, and do it on subscription, and people could download it? And two years down the line, you could do a compilation for those who wanted one.
Ed (2000)

If we choose to go off in a new direction and do something different, it's okay if you don't want to come along this time. But we'll probably be returning your way sometime anyway. We'll be getting our guitars out just when everyone else is doing German techno. So don't worry about us!
Thom (2001)

My plans for old age? Age badly. Follow random pathways in the forest. Smoke a pipe. Become a hermit. Never shave ever again. Take Ecstasy on weekends. Develop a Valium habit. Read the Bible. Go to Tibet. Become an MP. Change my name. Laugh at economists. Start skanking dancehall style.
Thom (2001)